11/00

The Stolen Blue

THE

STOLEN

BLUE

JUDITH VAN GIESON

University of New Mexico Press Albuquerque

The Stolen Blue by Judith Van Gieson

© Judith Van Gieson, 2000

Published by arrangement with Signet,

a division of Penguin Putnum, Inc.

First edition

Library of Congress Cataloging-in-Publication Data

Van Gieson, Judith, 1941–

The stolen blue : a Claire Reynier mystery / Judith Van Gieson.
— 1st ed.

   p.   cm.

  ISBN 0-8263-2233-6

  1. Rare books—Collectors and collecting—West (U.S.)—Fiction.
2. Women detectives—West (U.S.)—Fiction.   3. Book thefts—West
(U.S.)—Fiction.   I. Title.

  PS3572.A42224 S76   2000

  813'.54—dc21   99-050500

To Dominick

Thanks to Betty Parker and Robert R. White
for all the book talk.

CHAPTER ONE

A year before her marriage broke up, Claire Reynier began establishing credit in her own name, practicing tai chi, and playing computer solitaire. She discovered that there were three types of hands: the hand that started out promising but fizzled when the card she needed was buried under another card, the hand that started out hopeless and remained that way, and the hand that was a gift of the cards. In the latter case aces came early, and there was always a space for the kings. On rare occasions they could be won on the first pass through the deck, in which case her computer gave her thirty-five hundred bonus points. These games were difficult because each card could only be turned over once. The games Claire liked best started out badly but by a careful move—letting a black king go by, for example, while waiting for a red—could be rescued and won. She was in the middle of a hand with an uncertain outcome when Burke Lovell called her from his ranch house in the Blue.

"How are you, Burke?" she asked. The rumor had been circulating around the university library that he was not well.

"I'm havin' a little trouble breathin', that's all." His voice, which had once terrorized subordinates, was a hoarse whisper.

"Is it emphysema?" Preferable, Claire thought, to cancer, the other alternative. Burke had been a heavy smoker.

"Yeah. They got me on oxygen, but I can still play a hand of Texas Hold 'Em for all it's worth."

"I bet you can," Claire said.

"How's the new job going?" he asked her.

"Good. Thanks, Burke." The first résumé Claire sent out once she knew her marriage was terminal and she decided to leave Tucson went to Burke Lovell. He had hired her right out of library school and been her mentor when he was head of the Department of Southwest Studies at the University of Arizona. However, due to a cutback in funds, Burke had moved on to Albuquerque to the Center for Southwest Research at the University of New Mexico. He was a giant in his field. No one knew more about the books of the Southwest than Burke. Claire would have liked to have followed him when he went to UNM, but she had a husband in Tucson then and two children to raise. Burke was now retired, but he was still a powerful influence on the Center for Southwest Research. He had found an opening for Claire or caused one—she wasn't sure which—as the head of collection development. Basically her job was to buy books for the library, a dream spot; Claire liked nothing better than to search for rare books. Unfortunately, the librarian she replaced had been well liked in the department, and she had to tread carefully to be accepted.

"Do you like New Mexico?" he asked.

"I do." Evan, her ex-husband, thought it was a lawless, dirty state. But it had a frontier quality that appealed to Claire. It was a good place to start a new life. "It's cold, though. They have a real winter here." She looked out her window and saw snowpack on the mountains and a dusting on the ground. Every night she'd been burning piñon in her fireplace, but she never felt completely warm.

"It's been cold in the Blue, too," Burke said. "The reason I called, Claire, is I am going to turn my private collection over to UNM."

"All of it?"

"Yup. My kids don't give a damn." He paused to clear his throat. "You think you could drive over Saturday to pick it up?"

"Sure." Claire had no one to answer to now. Her son was in California and her daughter in Boston. Evan had a newer, younger wife. If she wanted to go to the Blue on two days' notice, she could go. If she wanted to eat popcorn for dinner and watch a video from bed, she could do that, too.

"Bring the truck," Burke said.

"Of course. See you Saturday."

"I'm looking forward to it."

Claire returned to her game, but in the course of her conversation with Burke, she had accidentally bumped the mouse and the computer had dealt a new hand.

Claire's truck was outfitted with four-wheel drive and a watertight camper shell; transporting rare and valuable book collections was a significant part of her job. Friday after work she loaded the bed with boxes, tape, and bubble wrap. She wanted to surprise her colleagues with Burke's collection and didn't tell anyone she was going to the Blue. It was a luxury after years of having to account for every minute of her time, but it was unnerving that she could disappear for a weekend with no one to notice her absence. The Blue was two hundred and twenty miles away, New Mexico miles with lots of beauty and little traffic. It was the kind of driving Claire enjoyed, and she didn't consider it a long trip.

When she got up Saturday morning, gray clouds had gathered around the mountains. She began the day by practicing tai chi meditation, standing with her feet together, closing her eyes, letting her hands fall loosely to her sides in the position known as the infinite ultimate stance. One reason Claire enjoyed tai chi was she liked the names of the positions. It also suited her better than sitting meditation; she didn't like sitting still. She put her weight on her left leg, shifted to her right, balanced on both raising her arms to chest level to form one open circle with her arms and another with the palms of her hands. She imagined she was balancing three balls: one between her knees, one in her arms, and the third between her fingertips. She stayed in this position for several minutes, trying to clear her mind of thought. When a practitioner remained still long enough, stillness led to movement. She returned to the infinite ultimate stance, rubbed her palms together until they were warm, and rested them on her eyes.

She finished by walking through her house followed by Nemesis, her cat, who wanted to be fed. The house was small and had a minimum of decoration. Claire worked with Southwestern art and artifacts all day; she had chosen not to live with them. Her carpet and upholstery were a plain, soft gray that she found restful.

She fed the cat and left the house. It was snowing again and starting to stick to the street. The air smelled of piñon. Her tires left tracks in the unmarked surface. Once she got to the interstate, however, traffic kept the road clear, a relief since Claire had little experience driving in snow. She took I-40 west and was struck by how drab New Mexico looked without the sun. Gray clouds sat on the horizon. The earth was a dull pink. The new developments under construction beside I-40 exposed their wooden ribs. Cars coming east from Grants or Gallup had their headlights on—a sure sign of bad weather. When she passed through the Laguna Reservation, Claire saw moisture evaporating from the fields and black cattle silhouetted in the mist. At the Stuckey's exit, she stopped to get coffee then turned south onto Route 117. As she drove past El Malpais National Monument, the clouds began to clear and the sun broke through, illuminating the red cliffs around La Ventana Natural Arch, showing the striations of color and time.

Claire was unlikely to see another car for seventy-five miles on this lonely stretch of highway. She put a favorite Mozart piano concerto into the tape deck, turned up the volume, and let the music fill the cab. She thought of Mozart as lush green music, but it played well in the desert. The beauty of the setting and the harmony of the music were turning this drive into a peak experience.

She'd been seeking peak experiences more since her father had died of Parkinson's disease. She'd searched the Internet for information about Parkinson's and read that the adrenal gland produces dopamine at moments of heightened pleasure or effort. It was a survival mechanism. Those who produced the most dopamine became the strongest, smartest, bravest, and most likely to survive. Her father's life had been strong on duty, but lacking in pleasure and adventure. Dopa had been the only drug that had helped him.

His death had been slow and difficult—not the way Burke Lovell or Claire herself would want to die.

She thought about Burke, a brilliant, demanding man whose life had been full of peak experiences, but whose heart had rarely gotten a workout. He'd ignored his children and treated the women he'd been involved with shabbily. He did best with students and protégés who were willing to reflect back his brilliance. Claire had known Burke for twenty-five years. He had started as her mentor, but along the way they'd become friends. Burke didn't have many close friends, and he valued the relationship with Claire.

The tape reversed itself. Claire left El Malpais and entered Catron County, cattle country, where the land had been grazed down to stubble. She drove through the sleepy village of Quemado. Sixty miles later she reached the county seat of Reserve. Residents of Reserve, proud of their reputation for being radical and ornery, celebrated the Fourth of July by shooting off their weapons. They tried to pass a law that a citizen was required to own a gun to live there. It was a deeply conservative area, so conservative it made Burke appear liberal, although no one at UNM ever believed that Burke was a liberal.

Claire went south on Route 180 until she came to Mile Marker 22 and the dirt road that descended into the Blue. Her work took her all over the Southwest, but she knew of no place like the Blue, a settlement of twenty families along the banks of the Blue River surrounded by hundreds of thousands of acres of national forest. You had to drive through twenty-five miles of forest to get to the valley on a white knuckle road full of switch backs, ruts, and deep drop-offs, which was exactly how the residents liked it. They made their living as ranchers grazing their cattle on public lands.

Property rarely changed hands in the Blue. Burke had inherited the ranch from his friend Benjamin deWitt. It was equidistant from Tucson and Albuquerque, and Claire had been there during both of Burke's tenures. It was an enchanted valley, a remote paradise as long as a person didn't have to live there alone. Claire was remembering how the valley looked in summer, the intense new greens, the dry dusty greens, when her thoughts were interrupted by a woman in a pickup truck with a rifle mounted across the rear window. The woman came barreling around a blind curve forcing Claire to pull into the side of the hill. The woman lifted a hand from the steering wheel in a casual cowboy wave.

Claire lifted a hand back and continued her descent. When she reached the river, she saw collars of ice circling the rocks. The elevation here was seven thousand feet, high enough to give the Blue a real winter. The bare limbs of cottonwoods curved and wandered across the valley like country roads. As she drove through the valley, Claire saw a number of metal mailboxes but few houses. Houses in the Blue tended to be hidden from the road. She crossed a bridge and pulled into Burke's place, a hotel-sized log cabin. Smoke rose from the chimney and drifted across the roof. Elk grazed in Burke's field. Usually elk didn't come this close in the afternoon, but in the winter forage was scarce.

Burke's daughter Corinne and his dog Roamer met her at the door. Whenever she encountered Burke's children, Claire thought of all the times a beautiful woman had a plain-looking daughter and how often a driven, successful parent had a dysfunctional child. Some law of compensation seemed to determine that a parent with too much drive stole the energy from the offspring. Burke's children weren't lacking in intelligence, but they all had problems functioning in the real world. Corinne had given up and moved into her father's house, where she acted as a housekeeper. She cooked for everyone in the house, but rarely took the time to feed herself. Corinne reminded Claire of a piece of dry and gnarled wood washed up beside a river. How old was she now? In her forties Claire guessed. She'd been a teenager when Burke was still at U of A. But her thinness and her poor posture made her look like an old woman. Her hair was pulled into a loose bun. She wore a faded dress and a baggy cardigan sweater with worn patches at the elbows.

"Good to see you," Corinne said, giving Claire a bony hug.

"You, too," Claire replied. She bent over to pet the dog, a hound with long, silky ears. "How's Burke doing?"

"You know my father. His lungs might be giving out, but his

mind is as sharp as ever. He's in the library playing poker with his nurse."

Claire followed Corinne down the hallway across the living room and into the library. When he first moved to the Blue, Burke went native briefly and became an enthusiastic hunter. His trophies were mounted on the living room's log walls: a monumental bison head, a javelina with a long snout, a white-tailed deer, and an elk. A fire burned in the massive stone fireplace, and the game stared at it with fixed and glassy eyes.

Another fire was burning in the woodstove in the library—Claire's favorite room in the house. Many people coveted Burke's ranch with its deep and total privacy, the river flowing by and the elk grazing in the fields. Guests fell in love with the place and never wanted to leave. For Claire, the jewel at the center of the property was the library with windows facing the meadow and floor-to-ceiling books, all of them interesting, many of them very rare. This room contained the story of the Southwest.

Burke sat beside the woodstove with a blanket across his lap and cards in his hand. The nurse, a stocky woman with skin like hide and faded blue eyes, sat on the other side of the stove. A young woman wearing hiking boots, jeans, and a plaid shirt stood beside Burke. Her porcelain skin contrasted with the dark sheen of her hair. A toddler wearing denim overalls trimmed in plaid played at her feet. He had his mother's fair skin and dark hair, but the roses in his cheeks were his own. Burke's oxygen tank was on the floor, and the tubes were hooked up to his nose. Roamer, the hound, followed them into the library and collapsed on the floor.

"You'll excuse me if I don't get up?" Burke asked Claire.

"Sure," Claire said. She bent over and kissed the top of his head. His white hair was thin, but his eyes were bright, as if they'd stared into the fire long enough to reflect back the flame.

"Kass is beating me again." He nodded at the nurse.

"No way. You play this game?" she asked Claire. "I could use some relief."

"Not very well," Claire answered. "Lately I've been playing solitaire."

"She finally got rid of a no-good philandering husband," Burke said.

Takes one to know one, Claire thought. Her husband had only done it once that she'd been sure of, but Burke had been a repeat offender during his married years. "If you say so," she replied.

"I do." He sized her up. "You're still a good-looking woman, Claire. You'll find someone better."

Still? thought Claire. Burke showed no signs of introducing her, so she extended her hand to the nurse and then the young woman. "Claire Reynier," she said.

"Kassandra Wells," the nurse replied.

"Mariah Geraty." The young woman's gaze was steady and her handshake firm.

"Mariah is my long-lost daughter," Burke said. "And that's my grandson Eric." He smiled at Eric, and the little boy giggled.

"I didn't know you had another daughter or a grandchild, Burke," Claire said.

"Neither did I until Mariah tracked me down last year."

Mariah put her hand on Burke's shoulder, and he squeezed it tight. She was an attractive young woman who exuded confidence, the only one of Burke's descendants who appeared to have his drive. In his waning years fate had handed him a gift, Claire thought: a daughter that someone else had raised.

Burke waved his hand to dismiss his family and nurse. "Everybody out," he said. "I need to talk to Claire."

When she and Burke were alone, Claire settled into the chair that Kassandra had vacated.

"I've prepared an inventory of the books," he began.

There was a manila folder under the blanket on his lap. He pulled the inventory out of the folder and handed it to Claire. She glanced through it quickly. It was a collection any library would be proud to own, and it would be a coup for her to bring it in. Burke's collection would secure her position at the Center for Southwest Research, although it might also increase the level of resentment. "This is an incredible bequest, Burke. The library will be so pleased."

"You will make sure my name is on it," he said.

"Of course." Claire began making her way through the inventory beginning with "A" and the "Edward Abbeys." Abbey remained a hero to Burke and many men in the West, although in Claire's opinion his monkey wrench books were sophomoric. It was a subject she'd debated with Burke on occasion, but this didn't seem to be the right occasion. She noticed an error on the list. "You have a copy of *Black Sun* here signed and dated March, 1971." It wasn't Abbey's most valuable book, but it was Claire's favorite, a love story between a park ranger and a college student set deep in the canyons of Arizona.

"That's right," Burke said.

"No, it's not right. *Black Sun* was published in May, 1971 not in March."

"How could you possibly remember that?" Burke's eyes got a hard glaze when he tried to intimidate. "That book was published over twenty years ago."

"My son was born in May, and I reviewed the book for *Book Talk* after we got home from the hospital."

Age and illness had shortened Burke's fuse. "If I put March on that list, then that's what the inscription says," he snapped.

Claire didn't doubt it, but Edward Abbey had been known to sign books long after publication. If he signed a copy of *Black Sun* years later, he might not have remembered what month it came out. It wouldn't take away from the value of the book any. It might even increase it. Book collectors valued idiosyncrasies and errors.

"I haven't lost my marbles yet," Burke barked, reminding Claire that the voice is the first weapon of the young and the last of the old. There were times when Burke's tone grated, but today she was relieved it hadn't lost its edge. "Although there's no telling how long that will continue." His voice slowed and drifted toward the sad no-man's-land Claire's father had inhabited in the latter stages of his illness when his mind began erasing its tracks. "I want to get my affairs in order while I am still able."

"You seem pretty able to me," Claire replied.

"Well, that won't last forever. After I completed the inventory, I decided to draw up a will. If I left my affairs to my children, that would be a sorry mess." He opened the folder that lay in his lap. "I've made you my personal representative. I need someone I can trust to carry out my wishes. My offspring," he sighed, "would never get it right." A log in the woodstove crackled and snapped. The dog lay its head on its paws and stared at the fire.

"All right," Claire said.

"As soon as this is witnessed, it will be valid; I used a program to prepare it on the computer. I see no point in wasting my money on a Catron County lawyer. I'm leaving the ranch to Mariah with the provision that Corinne can live here for the rest of her life. Corinne's gotten agoraphobic. She can hardly leave the house."

"She needs to eat something," Claire said, a mother's response.

"Corinne eats what she wants to eat. When it comes to stubbornness, she takes after me."

"What happens to Corinne if Mariah sells the property?"

"She can't. She has a life estate. As long as she or her heirs are willing to run it as a nature preserve, the ranch is theirs. If her heirs should decide to sell the place, it goes to the Nature Conservancy. We've stopped grazing cattle here to make room for the elk, and when the wolves come back I hope to see them here, too. Nothing gives me more pleasure these days than watching the wildlife, and that's a pleasure Mariah shares with me. I've given my grazing allotment back to the BLM. For as long as she lives, Mariah will run the ranch as a nature preserve. If I left it to my children, they'd either graze the hell out of it or sell it to developers."

"Your neighbors won't be happy about the nature preserve."

"The hell with my neighbors." Burke leaned forward, opened the door to the woodstove, and threw a log on the fire. "They like to wrap themselves in the flag and brag about how American they are, but their view of America doesn't allow for dissent. Mariah can handle them. What do they have to complain about anyway? All I'm doing is letting the property revert to the way it used to be."

"What about your other children?" Burke had a son, James, in Phoenix and a daughter, Samantha, in Santa Fe.

"They'll all get what I got when my father died—two hundred thousand each. I'd like to see if they can do as well with it as I did."

"They won't be happy with that, Burke. The ranch is worth a million or more."

"Since the ranch isn't going to be sold, the value is not an issue. It's too late now to change things with my children. When I look in their eyes, I see blame; when I look in Mariah's, I see a future. I've left the remainder of my liquid assets—two hundred thousand—to her. If there's a lawsuit, she'll have some cash to pay the legal fees and to negotiate with. As for the rest of them, I trust you'll keep the terms of the will quiet until the time comes."

"If that's what you want."

"It is." Burke rang the bell on the end table. "We need to get this thing witnessed. After that I'm taking a nap. It was a pleasure accumulating all this property, but deciding what to do with it wears me out." He sank back in his chair and breathed in some oxygen.

Kassandra came to the door. "Would you bring Jed in?" Burke asked.

"He's my ranch hand," he told Claire. While they waited for the witnesses, they worked their way through the inventory.

Kassandra returned with Jed, a wiry, dark-haired man in his forties who—to Claire—had the look of someone who'd spent too much time alone. He kept his eyes averted and seemed to be wrapped in a blanket of space.

When Burke asked him to witness the will, Jed said, "Sure, boss," and signed without giving the document a glance, although Kass dawdled as if she wanted to understand what she was signing. When they were done, Burke said, "Now, you all agree that I am of sound mind?"

They did. Burke put one copy of the will in his folder and handed the other to Claire. He stuck the folder under his arm and asked Kass to help him to his room. He walked slowly, leaning on Kass's arm and pulling the oxygen tank behind him. Roamer followed, scratching the wooden floor with his claws. "We'll see you at dinner," Burke said.

Claire spent the rest of the afternoon contentedly packing books and listening to the fire snap and hiss. As she took each book from the shelf, she balanced it carefully in her hands, giving it the atten-

11

tion something rare and valuable deserved. Many of Burke's books were in collector's condition, meaning both the book and dust jacket were flawless. Burke's books did not have price-clipped corners, library stamps, or the owner's name written on the endpapers. Some of the books had never been opened. Claire checked each book against the inventory and placed it in a box cushioned with bubble wrap. After she filled a box, she taped it shut with clear sealing tape, numbered it, and labeled it. A book she thought particularly interesting or valuable went into a separate box to show her colleagues, since the remainder of the collection was likely to sit in backlog until it could be cataloged.

She began with the Abbeys, making a mental note to check the inscription in *Black Sun* against a bibliography she had in the library. She put that book and *The Brave Cowboy,* Abbey's scarcest title, in a special box. The other Abbeys went into a box labeled *A.* One problem with finding Abbeys in good condition was that his readers were likely to throw them in a backpack and read them around a campfire before passing them along to their friends. Burke's copy of *The Brave Cowboy* was the only one Claire had ever seen in a fine dust jacket. She thought of it as the twenty-five hundred dollar dust jacket because the book was worth thirty-two hundred dollars with it, seven hundred dollars without. Inscribing a book to someone could decrease its value, but this book had a dream inscription because Abbey had inscribed it to Burke, who in some circles was as renowned as Abbey was.

Burke also collected ephemera and had a hard-to-find copy of *The Thunderbird,* the student newspaper Abbey edited when he was at UNM, in which he had attributed a quote from Voltaire to Louisa May Alcott. That quote—"Man shall not be free until the last general is strangled with the entrails of the last priest"—cost Abbey his position as editor.

Claire continued working her way through the alphabet to the accompaniment of the crackling fire. She set aside an unnumbered binder's copy of *Taos Pueblo* with text by Mary Austin and photographs by Ansel Adams. The photos had the exquisite, luminescent quality of Adams's black-and-white work. It was the gem of

Burke's collection. Not long ago Sotheby's had sold one for thirty thousand dollars. Very few of them existed outside of museums.

Rudolfo Anaya's *Bless Me Ultima* also went into the special box and Richard Bradford's *Red Sky at Morning*. The Bradford had never become very valuable, but it was a book that Claire admired. From the "C's" she added a signed and numbered limited edition of Willa Cather's *Death Comes for the Archbishop*. Periodically Claire looked out the window and noticed the lengthening afternoon shadows. Just before dark she saw a bull elk standing and studying the light from across the field in a posture of total alertness.

When Corinne called her to dinner, she made a quick estimate of how much wrapping and boxing lay ahead and saw several hours. They sat down in the dining room at a long table under a chandelier made of elk antlers. Jed joined them, but Kass had gone home. Burke poured them each a shot of Jack Daniel's. The only time Claire got drunk during her divorce proceedings had been on Jack Daniel's. She considered it a poisonous, seductive drink, and she sipped warily. Corinne had prepared beef stew and a chocolate cake for dessert. Claire thought the stew was subtly spiced and delicious, but Burke doused his with salt and layered it with grated pepper. Throughout the meal, he passed pieces of meat to the dog lying under the table. Corinne picked at her food, and when she served the chocolate cake, she didn't cut a piece for herself. It takes a rare person, Claire thought, to bake a chocolate cake and not eat any.

Burke appeared tired during dinner and said little. Claire tried to make conversation with Mariah by telling her about her son, who was in the computer business in Silicon Valley, and her daughter, who was teaching in Boston. Claire was struck by the contrast between her own children who had been so eager to leave Arizona and get out into the world and Mariah who seemed content to have retreated into the Blue. Eric was well behaved during dinner, which Claire considered a sign of good parenting.

After dinner Mariah took Burke back to his bedroom, and Claire returned to the library, where she stoked the fire and boxed books. Around eleven she realized how stiff and sore she was getting. She stood up, stretched, and went to bed in the downstairs guest room. Burke's door was open, and she noticed that his TV was turned to the weather channel. He appeared to have fallen asleep. She thought about turning the TV off, but didn't want to wake him.

Someone—probably Burke—had taken the trouble to assemble the head of a jackalope—a jackrabbit with antlers—and hang it on the wall of the guest room. Claire was too tired to appreciate the humor. She fell asleep immediately, but was awakened later by something she could only describe as deep silence. She sensed a change in atmosphere, got up, and went to the window. Three inches of snow had fallen, giving the cactus cone-shaped hats. The snow on the ground was a smooth white blanket as far as she could see. She went back to the warm bed and pulled up the covers.

When she woke again at dawn, Corinne was standing in the doorway. "My father is gone," she said in a tight voice.

Claire sat up. "He must be in the bathroom. Where else could he go with his oxygen tank?"

"I already checked the bathroom, and he didn't take his oxygen tank. It's still in his bedroom."

"Oh, God," Claire said. She got up, stepped into her shoes, wrapped her robe tight, and followed Corinne through the first floor of the house. Corinne turned the lights on in each room they entered, and left them burning after they'd completed their search. She wore a robe with loose sleeves that fell away as she flipped the switches. Claire noticed that her arms were scratched as if she'd just walked through a berry patch. There was no sign of Burke on the first floor. Claire thought of Alzheimer's patients who became confused and wandered away, but Burke's mind had seemed too sharp for that. They came to the foot of the stairs, and Corinne started to climb.

"Would Burke have been able to get up the stairs?" Claire asked.

"My father can be very determined," Corinne said.

Claire followed her to the second floor. There were several identical bedrooms with twin beds covered by Pendleton Indian blankets and a nightstand between them holding a lamp with a rawhide shade and a wrought-iron base. The first few rooms they entered were empty.

"Where does Jed sleep?" Claire asked.

"He has a trailer."

They came to the door of Mariah's room, and Corinne knocked. When there was no answer, she pushed open the door and switched on the light. Eric was sleeping in a crib. The sheets on Mariah's bed were turned down, the blanket was gone, the bed was empty. Roamer, who had been tagging along behind them, started to howl, and they heard the front door at the foot of the stairs open. They hurried to the stairwell and saw Mariah standing in front of the open door wrapped in a blanket wet with snow, and holding another blanket in her arms.

"What's happened to my father?" Corinne cried.

Mariah waited for them to descend the stairs, then said in a voice that was unnaturally calm, "He's dead." Her eyes under the hood of the blanket had a dark glow.

"How did he die? Where is he?" Corinne demanded.

"He's under the cottonwood tree by the river. It was how he wanted to die outside in the snow."

"He didn't . . ." Claire wasn't able to finish the sentence, but Mariah knew what she meant. The way men in the West who kept guns usually killed themselves was with a bullet through the head.

"No," Mariah answered. She dropped the blankets to the floor and shook the snow from her hair. Claire circled behind her, closed the door, picked up the blankets, and put them on a chair. "He died of exposure," Mariah continued. "He wanted to do it on the coldest night so it would be quick, and he liked the idea of doing it in the snow. He told me that last night was a good night to die." She turned toward Claire. "He said to tell you he's sorry it had to happen when you were here."

"You helped my father to die?" Corinne asked.

"It was what he wanted, Corinne. He hated the thought of losing his mind and turning into a vegetable in a nursing home. He was ready. It was better for him to go this way."

"How did he get to the cottonwood?"

"I helped him."

"And then you just left him there?"

"He took some Valium and curled up in the snow. He asked me to remove the blanket once he went to sleep and then to leave him alone. I waited near the river so I could hear if he woke up or cried out, but he never did."

Claire wouldn't deny that this was a death Burke might have chosen, but it took a cold person to be as matter-of-fact about it as Mariah was. She must be in shock, Claire thought. She was seeing signs of it in herself, a detached sensation as if she were floating above the room and watching from the ceiling.

Corinne demanded to be taken to the body. Claire had to remind her to put on boots and a jacket. She got dressed, Mariah threw her blanket back on, and they stepped outside. The fields were getting light, although the woods were still in deep shadow. The snow had stopped falling. One set of tracks was visible in the smooth white surface—Mariah's hiking boots leading to the house. They followed the tracks back to the cottonwood, a magnificent tree ten feet thick with a textured trunk and enveloping arms. Burke's body, in a pair of thin cotton pajamas, lay under it. His lips were blue, and his skin was as white as marble. He was obviously dead, but Claire knelt down and felt for the carotid artery to be sure. There was no pulse, and his skin had the texture of packed snow.

"He didn't suffer," Mariah said.

"You should put a blanket over him," said Corinne.

What difference does it make now? Claire thought. He's dead.

She believed they should leave him exactly as he was and call the sheriff, but Mariah took her blanket off and laid it over Burke. The blanket leant him some dignity and calmed Corinne, but Mariah, who was wearing a cotton nightgown, began to shiver without it. Claire took her back to the house while Corinne stayed under the tree, keeping a vigil beside the body of her father.

Jed, who was waiting when they got back to the porch, swore softly when Claire told him about Burke. "Anything I can do?" he asked.

"Keep an eye on Corinne while I call the family and the sheriff," Claire replied.

"Sure," he said.

He headed for the cottonwood tree, Mariah went upstairs to her room, and Claire went into the kitchen and made a pot of coffee before she made her calls. She found the numbers she needed in an address book beside the phone. The sheriff said he'd get there as soon as he could, but the roads were slick this morning. Next she called Burke's children. Samantha's answering machine said to leave the date and time of the message. Claire was relieved to get the machine; she found Samantha difficult in the best of times. James was stunned and said he would come over right away. Claire knew it was a five-hour drive from Phoenix, which would make it mid-afternoon before James reached the Blue. She hoped the sun would come out and clear the roads by then. She called out the door to Corinne and Jed that coffee was ready, but they didn't answer. She poured a cup for herself, took it to the library with Roamer tagging along behind her, sank into a deep armchair, and stared out the window, overwhelmed with sadness, numbed by the enormity of her loss.

CHAPTER TWO

When she heard a vehicle pull into the driveway forty-five minutes later, Claire went to the front door expecting the sheriff, but finding the nurse Kassandra Wells letting herself in. "You're here early," Claire said, thinking how irrelevant the comment was even as she said it. A part of her brain sought refuge in the trivial and the normal.

"Same time as I always get here," Kass replied taking her jacket off and hooking it over the coatrack. Her hair was windblown, and her cheeks were burning from the cold.

"Where do you live?" Claire asked, postponing the inevitable.

"Reserve."

"That's a long drive to make every day."

Kass shrugged. "I'm used to it."

"How were the roads?"

"Not too bad." She finger-combed her hair into place and prepared to go to work. "How's Burke this morning?"

"I'm very, very sorry to have to tell you this, Kass, but Burke died during the night."

"Burke died? How did that happen?"

"Exposure."

"Now, how the hell did Burke die of exposure?" Kass focused her faded blue eyes on Claire. "He was safe and warm when I left him."

"He went outside in the middle of the night and went to sleep under the cottonwood tree. He left his oxygen tank behind him." It occurred to Claire that was more or less how Edward Abbey had tried to end his life, but he hadn't succeeded. Abbey had gone out into the desert, but it hadn't been winter and he hadn't been seventy-five years old, either. Abbey had ended up dying in his own bed a victim of cirrhosis of the liver.

"Burke didn't get out there by himself, did he?"

"Mariah helped him. She said he told her last night was a good night to die. Apparently, he thought it would be quicker in the snow."

"Burke could have gone on for years the way he was. His mind was clear, he was well fed and taken care of, he wasn't an Eskimo who has to go out and die in the snow. He lived in this beautiful place surrounded by women who loved him, what's so bad about that? I've seen many people who were a lot worse off than Burke Lovell. You don't take your life just because it's not on your own terms anymore. What the hell's wrong with Mariah helpin' him die like that? Hasn't that girl got any conscience or any sense?"

Claire was relieved she wouldn't have to answer that question because at that moment Sheriff Henner arrived in a white and blue county car. She hadn't decided whether Burke's death was a matter of conscience or of courage. She had often wondered whether she would have had the courage to help her father die if he had asked her to, but he never did. He just grew weaker and sadder and more dependent.

Claire let the sheriff and his deputy in. Henner was a big man, wearing jeans and boots and a sheepskin vest. He had long legs and a stomach that sagged across his belt buckle. There were deep vertical creases in his cheeks connected by horizontal creases across his forehead and the middle of his chin. Even when his eyes and mouth smiled, the lines locked his face into a puzzled frown. He took off his cowboy hat. "Morning, ladies."

"Morning," Claire answered.

"I'm Sheriff Henner. This here is Deputy Johnson."

"Mornin'," the deputy said. He was younger and fairer than the weathered sheriff.

19

"How you doin', Kass?" the sheriff asked.

"Been better."

"It could be worse," Henner replied. "Too often when I get these kinds of calls the man has blown his brains all over the map. Well . . ." He put his hat back on. "You mind showin' me where the body is?"

Claire put on her coat and led the sheriff, the deputy, and Kass out to the cottonwood. The once-smooth snow was now criss-crossed by footprints. Corinne had cleared some ground under the tree and sat there hugging her knees trembling like the lone leaf on an aspen branch at the end of the season. Jed was hunkered down beside her.

"I'm real sorry about this, Corinne," Henner said, patting her arm and bending over to take a closer look at the body.

The red blanket that spread out around Burke resembled a blood-stain, brilliant against the white snow. Claire wished there were some way a person could die and take his body along with him. A body shouldn't be left behind to be poked and prodded and re-membered like this. Death ought to be a black hole that you stepped into and pulled your physical being behind, stretching it out until it became thin and ephemeral as a cobweb.

Kass stared at Burke and shook her head. "It didn't have to end this way," she said.

Sheriff Henner stood up. "The ambulance will be here soon. You sure you don't want to come inside, Corinne?"

"I'll wait here."

"I'll stay with her," Jed offered.

"Deputy Johnson will keep you company," Henner said.

While Claire walked the sheriff and Kass back to the house, she noticed Mariah watching them from an upstairs window, holding Eric in her arms.

"That's the other daughter?" the sheriff asked Claire. "The one you told me helped Burke to die?"

"Yes."

"I'll need to talk to her and you. Kass, you stick around, too. I know you weren't here when it happened, but you were taking care of him, weren't you?"

"Tryin' to," Kass said.

The sheriff set up headquarters in the kitchen with a pot of coffee at his elbow. He took out a pen and placed a pad on the kitchen table. Claire went upstairs and told Mariah that Henner wanted to talk to her. Mariah came down dressed in jeans and the same plaid shirt she'd worn the night before. She gave Eric to Kass to watch. Claire introduced her to the sheriff, then went back to the library. As she passed Burke's room, she saw Kass sitting in an armchair staring vacantly out the window. Eric was on the floor playing with a truck. Roamer had curled up on Burke's bed looking guilty and forlorn.

Claire started a fire in the woodstove in the library. There was an iciness inside her that only a fire could melt. She was staring at the flames when Mariah came to the door to say it was her turn to be interviewed.

The coffee was gone, so Claire brewed another pot, then sat down at the table across from the sheriff. The sun had come out, and the snow was melting and dripping from the eaves.

"Mariah tells me she went to check on Burke in the middle of the night, and that's when he asked her to take him outside," Henner began. "She says she doesn't know exactly what time that was. Did you hear anything?"

"No," Claire replied. "I woke up at some point, but the house seemed very quiet to me. I went to the window. It was snowing and starting to stick, but I didn't see any prints in the snow."

"Mariah says this was a plan she and Burke hatched between themselves. Any idea why they put this plan into effect last night?"

"Burke thought he'd die faster in the snow?"

"It didn't have anything to do with your being here did it?"

"Not to my knowledge."

"You and Burke go back a long time?"

"A long time. Twenty-five years."

The sheriff put his pen down and studied Claire. Although his eyes were kindly, his face fell into the creases of a frown. "Why were you here?"

"Burke called and asked me to come over. He was donating his rare book collection to the library at UNM where I work."

"He just wanted you to pick up the books?"

"Yes, but he also made me his personal representative in his will. He signed it yesterday and had Kass and Jed witness his signature."

"Looks like he got his ducks all in row before he took his life." Henner wrapped his hand around the pen and resumed taking notes in a script that resembled toy soldiers marching in formation across the page. "You didn't see this coming?"

"No."

"You mind telling me what the will says? It's gonna be public property as soon as it gets filed anyway."

Claire did mind, but figured she had no choice. "Some money goes to the children, the ranch goes to Mariah, with the provision that Corinne can continue living here."

"This is a valuable property for a woman as young as Mariah to be inheriting. What does she know about ranching?"

"It's not going to be a ranch anymore. It's going to be a nature preserve. The only way it can ever be sold is to the Nature Conservancy."

The sheriff put his pen down. "Burke's lettin' the Nature Conservancy into the Blue? The neighbors sure as hell won't like that."

"Only if Mariah's heirs decide to sell. The ranchers around here are likely to be long dead before the Nature Conservancy gets it."

"Well, their children won't be dead and their children's children won't be dead." The Blue was a place where people thought about what would be happening to their grandchildren sixty years down the road. "You'll be getting me a copy of that will?"

Claire said she would. She heard the ambulance wailing as it came down the hill. The siren struck her as excessive, since the road could hardly be full of vehicles to warn away.

"Just a few more questions, ma'am," the sheriff brought her attention back to the matter at hand. "Do you believe Burke was a man who was capable of planning his own death?"

"I do."

"And that death is the one he would have planned?"

"I believe so," Claire said.

The siren alerted the neighboring ranchers who began arriving in their pickup trucks and gathering in the dining room. The sheriff interviewed Kass and Jed. Claire went into the kitchen and helped Corinne heat up the leftover stew. She was surprised by how hungry she was, until she remembered she hadn't eaten anything all day. They put out the stew, and people began helping themselves from a serving dish on the dining room table.

A young couple stood beside the table, and Corinne introduced them as Karen and Orin Stoner, the owners of the adjacent ranch. Their youth and good health made Corinne seem even more frail. Karen's curly blonde hair was held in place with beaded barrettes. She wore stiff new jeans belted tight at the waist. Orin had a broad-shouldered, narrow-hipped cowboy build. He wore black jeans and a gray Western shirt reverse appliquéd with black and white diamonds. His dark eyelashes emphasized his pale eyes, the eyes of a pilot or a quarterback that seemed focused on long distance. His cool manner indicated he was used to being looked up to. Claire knew that large landowners were considered aristocracy in small Western towns. For many people the role of rancher was an enviable one, a life spent outdoors without apparent compromise.

"How long have you been in the Blue?" Claire asked them.

"All my life," Orin answered. "I'm the fourth generation to run the Black Diamond."

"You're running it already?"

"Yes, ma'am," he replied.

"Orin's dad died last year in a plane crash," Karen said, hooking her arm through his. "That's when we inherited the Black Diamond."

"You're a friend of Burke's?" Orin asked Claire.

"We worked together for years."

"You didn't play cards together, did you?"

"Not me. I'm not in Burke's league."

"Me, neither," Orin laughed. "But that didn't stop me from playing him. Good thing I never bet the ranch. Now, I didn't always agree with Burke . . ."

Who did? Claire wondered.

"But he was my neighbor. We got along." Roamer padded into the room, flopped down beside Burke's chair, and rested his head on his paws. "That dog's not going to be worth a damn without Burke. Never was much of a hunter anyway. Burke used to hunt with my dad when he first moved down here, but his heart wasn't in it. We gave him Roamer when we saw he wasn't going to work out for us. I hear Burke was talking about giving up his grazing rights and turning this place into some kind of nature preserve. You know if there's any truth in that?" The pale eyes lost their remoteness as they focused on Claire, making her—for a moment—the most important person in the room.

"You'd have to ask the family about their plans." Corinne, the only family member present, had sat down at the far end of the table and was picking at her stew.

"Have you ever been on a working ranch?" Orin asked.

"It's been awhile," Claire said.

"Stop by and see us before you go," said Karen.

"I'd like that," Claire replied, but her thoughts were on getting back to Albuquerque.

Mariah came into the dining room, followed by Eric, who was clutching a toy truck. She nodded curtly to the Stoners and helped herself to a bowl of stew.

"Hi, darlin'," Karen said to Eric.

"Hi," the little boy replied.

"So sorry about your father, Mariah. I know how much you'll miss him." Karen's voice dripped honey, but underneath the smoothness Claire detected a burr.

"Thanks," Mariah said. She took her stew in one hand and Eric in the other, and went back upstairs.

When she finished eating, Claire returned to the library. She had already emptied the top shelves and began working her way through the "H's", the Tony Hillermans, the Dorothy Hughes, taking comfort in the rhythm of the work. She was expected back at the library on Monday for a meeting, and she had decided to return, thinking it might be good for the family to be alone together in their grief.

She wrapped the most valuable Hillerman, a first edition of his first mystery, *The Blessing Way,* signed before his angular signature had been smoothed out by years of signings. That book had a minuscule first printing, and Claire had recently seen one in mint condition priced at two thousand dollars. She put *The Blessing Way* into the box she was setting aside, along with a copy of *A Thief of Time,* her favorite Hillerman, illustrated on the title page by the Navajo artist Ernest Franklin. Claire liked Franklin's illustrations, but his Leaphorn and Chee didn't resemble her Leaphorn and Chee. She was aware that the books she valued most were fiction and modern firsts, and that if Burke had been doing the choosing, there would have been more history. She came across a local history mis-shelved in the "H's", and not wanting to pack it out of sequence, she set it aside.

She added Dorothy Hughes's *Ride the Pink Horse* and John Nichols's *Milagro Beanfield War* to her special box. The Hughes was printed in the forties on cheap wartime stock that turned paper-bag brown as it aged. It had never become very collectible, but it was a book Claire admired. She was called out of the library again in midafternoon when Burke's son, James, arrived with his wife. Claire hadn't seen James for years and had never met his current wife. When he was a teenager, James had been diagnosed as a manic depressive and put on lithium. Claire had witnessed a psychotic episode the summer after his freshman year at the U of A when James believed he was Mark Spitz, the Olympic swimmer. He climbed up on top of a library table to accept his imaginary medals and succeeded in terrifying everybody else in the library and embarrassing the hell out of his father. He had been up for days, but no one could restrain him. His eyes were wide and full of pain, and to Claire it looked as if the color of the iris was bleeding into the white. James in a manic phase was a clock that was wound too tight. He went at twice the speed of everyone else. When he crashed, he became a passive animal. Medicine was a leveling influence, but manic depressives didn't always take it; they felt the highs were worth the lows. Claire didn't know how James was faring with the illness and the medication. It had been hard to get Burke to talk about him.

The James who arrived at the ranch seemed slower and heavier than the one Claire had known. His lips were thick, his eyes were dull, his stomach was paunchy. His hair was flecked with gray. He wore a navy blue running suit with red stripes down the sides. James had become a RV salesman, and he dressed the part. He introduced Claire to his wife, Laura, who also wore a running suit, although hers was powder blue. In spite of the casual outfit, Laura was carefully made up. Her hair was spun gold, sprayed into a neat helmet, a shape and color it took hours at the hairdresser to achieve. At first glance the hair gave her the appearance of being younger than James. But the lines that circled her neck said otherwise. Claire remembered Burke, telling her that Laura held an administrative job. It could be what James needed, a woman who was older and better organized to keep him on his medication.

"I'm so sorry about Burke," Claire said.

"It was a shock," James answered. "I guess I thought he'd live forever. It's easy to believe that about your parents."

"Burke mentioned you used to work together?" Laura asked.

"That's right."

"What brought you over here this weekend?"

"Burke donated his rare book collection to the library, and he asked me to pick up the books."

Mariah came downstairs alone to greet her half brother. "Eric is napping," she said, giving James a hug. Seeing them together, Claire could find no resemblance. Different mothers, she thought. Different genes, different ways of being. Mariah seemed ready to conquer the world. James was struggling to get by.

"Good to see you, Mariah," Laura said, enunciating carefully. "Even under these difficult circumstances."

"You, too," Mariah replied.

The women did not touch, maintaining a wary distance that seemed quivering with tension to Claire. She excused herself and went back to the library. By late afternoon, her back was stiff and sore, but she'd reached the "W's" and the end was near. Only the bottom shelves had any books left on them. One of Burke's most prized books was a two-volume first edition of *Ben Hur,* written by Lew Wallace when he was governor of the Territory of New Mexico and inscribed in gratitude to Pat Garrett, the sheriff who killed Billy the Kid. It was a copy notable more for its inscription than its literary content. In a series of letters, Wallace had pretended to befriend the Kid, but had actually betrayed him. Double-crosser, Claire thought, but that didn't make the book less valuable. Antiquarians know that qualities that seem despicable in life are often admired after death. She wrapped *Ben Hur* and placed it in her special box.

When she finished the alphabet, she picked up the book that had been mis-shelved, a self-published history of the Blue by Benjamin deWitt, the rancher who left the ranch to Burke. Claire checked it against the inventory, but couldn't find an entry for it. The history was a slim jacketless volume, a little brown bird in a collection of peacocks. She looked up to see James standing in the doorway.

"It seems so empty in here without the books," he said. As he walked across the floor, the sound of his footsteps echoed in the depleted room. He sat down and draped his arms over the side of the chair. "What do you think about the way my father died?"

"I think he would have hated dying by inches in a nursing home," Claire replied, choosing her words carefully.

"Couldn't he have left us a note?"

In a way he had, Claire thought. His will said what Burke wanted to say. Eventually, she would have to relay the contents of the will to his heirs, but she didn't think that now, when their grief was so raw and new, was the moment.

"Why didn't he talk to me first?" Claire heard petulance in James's voice. "I would have liked to have had just one good conversation with my dad before he died. Just one."

Claire was relieved there had been no unfinished business with her own father. The thoughts left unsaid gave death a ragged edge.

"He didn't tell me he was leaving his books to the library, either," James continued.

Claire had always known James to be more interested in cars than he was in books. Nevertheless she said, "If there's anything you want, tell me," handing him the inventory. "The ones I've checked are in here." She indicated the special box. "The others are boxed alphabetically."

While James glanced through the list, she put *The History of the Blue* into the special box, which had space for another book, thinking that Burke would be pleased to know that she had included at least one history. Claire laid *Taos Pueblo* on top of the other books, closed the box, and taped it shut.

James put the list down without choosing a single title. "Would you pick one out for me?"

"When I get back to the library, all right?"

"All right," James said. "When do you leave?"

"As soon as I pack the truck. I have to get back for a meeting tomorrow."

"I'll help you take the boxes out."

"Thanks. Has Samantha arrived yet?"

"She'll be here later tonight. She was out of town and didn't get our messages till this afternoon."

The sense of relief she felt embarrassed Claire. To compensate, she said, "I'll get in touch with her when she gets back to Santa Fe."

"Are these ready to go?" James nodded toward the boxed books. "Yes."

"I'll start taking them out for you."

"Thanks. There's a hand truck in my pickup."

Claire wrote "VALUABLE" on the special box, carried it out herself, and put it on the passenger's seat. She helped James arrange the other boxes in the bed of the truck, then went inside to say her good-byes. Another rancher had arrived, older and softer than the wiry Orin Stoner. He was balanced on the edge of a dining room chair with his cowboy hat on his lap, talking to Sheriff Henner. The sheriff thanked Claire for her cooperation.

"Do you have to go so soon?" Corinne said.

"I have to be at the library for a meeting tomorrow. Let me know what the funeral plans are, and I'll come back. Your father was a brilliant man, Corinne, and a wonderful mentor to me. We're so lucky to have had him in our lives. I know how much you are going to miss him. We all will."

"Thanks," Corinne said, giving her a hug that left Claire with the sensation of having been embraced by a gnarled piece of wood.

"Are you going to drive all the way to Albuquerque tonight?" Laura asked. The lights had come on inside the house, turning the world beyond the windows a featureless black.

"If I get tired, I'll stop somewhere," Claire said.

"Why not just leave in the morning? There's plenty of room here." Laura stood next to James and was absentmindedly rubbing the small of his back.

"I think it would be good for all of you to be alone together."

"Let me know about the book," James said.

"I will."

"Have a good trip." Mariah offered a firm handshake. Eric was beside her, and Claire was tempted to pick him up and give him a hug. He was the kind of child who inspired that reaction. Claire's son had been like that, and she knew how damaging all the attention could be, so she just said, "Good-bye, Eric."

"Bye," the boy replied.

She was still surprised by Mariah's composure. She needed to let go and have a good cry. They all did. Maybe when everybody else left, they would find a way to be a family together in their grief.

The headlights of her truck led her up the tortuous dirt road. At one point she stopped at a lookout to peer back into the Blue and saw a crescent moon hanging over the valley. The air was cold and so still that the smoke from the chimneys rose straight up. By the time she reached Quemado, she was too tired to go any farther and she checked into a motel.

She brought in the special box, put it down on one of the twin beds, and headed for the bathroom. The dressing room beside the bath had a plastic countertop beneath a wall-to-wall mirror. Claire studied herself in the mirror, wondering if recent events had left a mark. She could use a good cry herself, but she hoped to postpone it until she got home. Her eyes had a startled, deer-in-the head-lights expression. Her chin seemed to have dropped a little lower. She took pride in her posture, and didn't like the way she had sunk into a slouch. She lifted her shoulders and straightened her back.

She remembered Burke's remark and wondered whether she was still a good-looking woman, whether she had ever been a good-looking woman, whether it mattered after she turned fifty. Sometimes she thought she'd married too young to find out how good-looking she was. Her layer of baby fat had lasted through high school. Only after she entered college did it fall away and reveal the fine bones in her face and her body. She had begun to discover there was power in her looks when she met Evan, who had subtle ways of turning her wattage down. Her clothes became more sub-dued after she got involved with him. She stopped lightening her hair. She became a wife, a librarian, and a mother with a quiet, professional style. Her purpose, as she saw it, was to support, not to attract. But she had remained thin. Her face was symmetrical, she had high cheekbones, her eyes were the pale, speckled blue of a robin's egg. She wore her hair in bangs and a pageboy that fell softly around her neck.

At this point in life, how good she looked depended on the light. In a diffuse light her hair was blonde. In daylight it was silver. In soft light she had fine wrinkles. In hard light her face was a road map of an overcrowded city. Claire knew that the more expensive the hotel, the more flattering the light—or was it a better quality of mirror? She had only paid thirty dollars for this room, and she was getting what she paid for. She gave up, turned out the light, went to bed, and hugged her pillow in an attempt to fill the void she felt.

She woke up late not knowing for a minute where she was. That she was in a motel room (and a cheap one) was obvious. But where? Somewhere in the Southwest, she could tell by the trim on the fur-niture. She rarely left the Southwest, so that much would also be obvious. Then it came to her that she was in Quemado, and the rea-son she was in this room settled over her shoulders like a weighted cape. There was always a brief moment upon waking up, a little crack in the window of consciousness, before the problems of the day came in. The problem of this day was that Burke Lovell was dead. Claire needed to get to a meeting in Albuquerque, and she had several hours of driving time ahead of her. She peeked out through the curtains. At least it wasn't snowing.

CHAPTER THREE

On the drive back Claire reinserted Mozart into the tape deck. He was good for restoring feelings of predictability and order. When Claire was a student, she discovered she made fewer typing errors if she typed her papers to Mozart. She had read that the sound of one concerto was the equivalent of ten milligrams of Valium, but the effect on her was less soothing than clarifying.

As Burke's personal representative, she'd be walking through a minefield of unhappy heirs. She hadn't wanted to face the ramifications while she was at the ranch, but now that she was on the road, she had to admit that family members would be resentful about the terms of Burke's will and with reason. Still, his intentions were clear, and she had agreed to honor them. She looked at the box of books on the passenger's seat. The driver's seat was always kept in the most upright position, and she leaned against it.

Ordinarily Claire enjoyed being on the lonesome highway. Driving could be a pleasure when there were no other cars on the road, but she was worried about making it back to the library on time. In the wide-open spaces north of Quemado, she saw a sunbow, a streaky cloud reflecting all the colors of the rainbow like a diamond in the deep blue sky.

By the time she reached the red rocks of El Malpais, she felt she could handle the Lovell family. By the time she reached Albuquerque, she wasn't so sure. A semi had jackknifed on the West Mesa and held up traffic for nearly an hour.

When she got to the library, she parked in her assigned spot and checked her watch. Director Hough's meetings always started on time, and the accident had made her late. She locked the books in the truck, hurried inside, and let herself into the conference room through the back door. She took the only empty seat at the table, too close to Hough's chair for her liking. He paused, from whatever he was saying, long enough to let her—and everybody else at the table know she was late.

"Sorry," she mumbled. She had good reason to be late and she might have taken this moment to blurt it out, but she wasn't prepared to be the center of attention or to interrupt the flow of the meeting. There was a prior agenda that Claire preferred to follow.

She had been put in charge of the exhibition room at the center and was expected to present the plans today for her first exhibit. In a drawer in the tower, she had come across an outstanding collection of Eliot Porter photographs. Porter had a gift for seeing patterns in the details of nature and Claire admired his work. To keep his photographs hidden in a drawer struck her as a waste.

"I think we should devote the next exhibit to the Eliot Porter photos," she said when her turn finally came.

"Do we have adequate security?" Ruth O'Connor, the senior member of the department, asked. Ruth reminded Claire of a little brown bird, her plumage was nondescript, but her eyes shimmered behind the thick lenses of her glasses, and she had a lyrical voice that sang the most ordinary words. Ruth had been widowed recently after a long marriage and was doing better than anyone expected.

"I'll look into it," Claire replied.

"Irina's exhibits were always of a historical nature," Harrison Hough said.

And duller than dishwater, thought Claire. Irina was her predecessor. If she had always done something, Claire thought that was reason enough to change the policy.

"You haven't seen them yet, have you, Harrison? They're exceptional." Ralph Monroe brushed away the sandy hair that had fallen

33

across his forehead. He was the kid in the department, earnest, honest, working on his Ph.D. in anthropology. "They'll bring in a lot of people."

"Do we want to bring in a lot of people?" queried Harrison. "This is a center for scholars, not an art gallery."

Claire suspected that if Burke had been sitting in that chair, he would have said go for it. Burke had been bold, Harrison was hesitant. Harrison was an administrator, not a trailblazer. Dealing with him resembled negotiating a shallow, rocky river in a tippy canoe. Claire was capable of doing it, but she resented the amount of effort and concentration it took.

"Why don't you take a look at the photos before you make a decision?" she asked, confident that the beauty of the work would win Harrison over. And, if he made the decision in his own office, he wouldn't appear to be backing down in front of his staff.

"All right," said Harrison, moving along to the next item on the agenda.

Celia Alegria, who tended to share Claire's enthusiasms, smiled at her from across the table. Celia had a radiant smile. Her surname meant joy, and it suited her. Celia liked to wear long skirts, boots, embroidered Levi jackets, and Guatemalan vests. It was a style that looked tired on many people, but she managed to keep it fresh. Claire always looked forward to seeing what Celia wore.

On the other hand, she never looked forward to seeing Gail Benton, also sitting across the table and stifling a yawn. Gail dressed drably—no color, no shape, no style. Her short brown hair should have been trim and neat, but she never seemed to get to the hairdresser on time. She was a tall woman who tried to appear shorter than she was by slouching and leaning.

What did I do now? Claire wondered. Had a good idea, she answered her own question.

While the meeting moved along, Claire wondered if Gail had wanted her job. Claire suspected that Gail made more money, but Claire's job was more interesting than manning the reference desk in the Anderson reading room. Gail might also resent the fact that, while she had a Ph.D. in American Studies, Claire's only postgraduate degree was an M.A. in Library Science. It took considerable drive to get a Ph.D. and that kind of ambition was often fueled by sibling rivalry. Ph.D.'s were frequently the eldest child, and Gail had three younger sisters whom she disliked intensely. Claire had been around universities long enough to know that there was often an inverse correlation between intellectual achievement and emotional maturity.

If she resents me now, she'll resent me even more when she hears I've brought in Burke's collection, Claire thought with a mixture of apprehension and pride. She waited until the business had been concluded and the staff members began gathering up their pens and notebooks, then she stood up and said, "I'm afraid I have some very bad news. Burke Lovell died over the weekend."

Her announcement fell like a large rock into a deep pond. The exclamations and questions splashed around her.

"Oh, no!"

"That's terrible."

"How did it happen?"

"It appears to have been a suicide," Claire said.

"How did he do it?"

"He disconnected his oxygen tank, took some Valium, went outside, and lay down in the snow."

"Why would Burke take his own life?"

"Apparently he wanted to die before he lost his faculties."

"That sounds like Burke."

"Was anyone with him?"

"His daughter, Mariah."

"I didn't know he had a daughter named Mariah."

"Neither did he until recently."

"What are the funeral plans?"

"I don't know yet."

"We should have a memorial service for him." ·

"We should."

"What will happen to his collection?" Harrison asked.

"He gave it to me for the library. The books are outside in my truck."

"That's wonderful. Burke's collection contains every book of historical or literary significance ever published about the Southwest," Harrison said.

"I set aside a box of special books to show you," Claire said.

"What did you put in it?" asked Ruth.

"*Bless Me Ultima, The Brave Cowboy,* a limited edition of *Death Comes for the Archbishop,* a copy of *A Thief of Time* illustrated by Ernest Franklin, and more."

"All novels?" queried Harrison.

"Mostly. I added a self-published history of the Blue and the limited edition of the Austin/Adams Taos Pueblo folio."

"We'll be one of a very few libraries to have one," Harrison beamed.

"I know."

"You must be very proud of yourself," said Gail, with the green-eyed monster dancing in her eyes.

"How wonderful for the library," Celia smiled.

"As you all know, it's an outstanding collection," Claire said.

"The best in the Southwest." Harrison turned the spotlight of his approval on her.

After the meeting, Claire invited Ruth into her office. Ruth perched on the edge of her chair and listened carefully.

"Burke made me his personal representative in his will," Claire said. "I don't know exactly what a personal representative does. I wondered if you had any experience with that when your husband died."

"Everything went to me and the children, so it wouldn't have been appropriate for me to be the personal representative. Robert asked his friend, Henry, to do that. Henry had to handle the expenses until the estate was probated. He hired a genealogical firm to search for unknown heirs who might have a claim to the estate. Now, in my husband's case, that was an easy job; there were none. But in Burke's . . ." She smiled and threw up her hands. "Have you seen the will yet?"

"Yes."

"Who got the ranch? There's a place people will be willing to do battle over."

"It's going to Mariah, the youngest daughter."

"Why her?"

"She shared Burke's interest in nature."

Ruth's eyes grew a little brighter, the lilt in her voice more pronounced. "And when did Burke get interested in nature?"

"Recently. Mariah has given Burke his only grandchild, a beautiful little boy named Eric."

"Well, you'll have your work cut out for you," Ruth said.

"What do you mean?"

"There are three other children, aren't there?"

"Right."

"They're liable to contest the will."

"I hope not," Claire replied.

"The will sounds like a recipe for trouble, but then Burke always did like trouble. May I offer some advice?" asked Ruth.

"Please."

"Hire a lawyer. The estate will pay the legal fees. With someone who led as complicated a life as Burke, settling his affairs is too much to ask of an amateur."

Claire hadn't been in Albuquerque long enough to know any lawyers. "Can you recommend someone?"

Ruth gave her the name of the lawyer Henry had used, and returned to her office. Claire called the lawyer, Sally Froelich, and made an appointment for later in the week. She went through the Eliot Porter folder on her desk and picked out a favorite print to show Harrison: an apple tree in the village of Tesuque, where Porter had lived. Claire hoped that at some point in her life she'd have the opportunity to live in a village, but the price of living in a New Mexico village was rising faster than her income. The photo was taken in late fall when the wind had stripped the tree branches bare, except for the apples that bobbed like golden ornaments against a misty gray background. She took the print into Harrison's office.

"I'm looking forward to seeing Burke's books," he said.

"You've never seen them?"

"No," Harrison sighed, reinforcing Claire's opinion that Burke didn't think much of him. Burke had shown *her* the collection many times. Harrison had been next in line when Burke retired, and he was the deans' choice for the job. Harrison was cost-conscious, which the administration considered important after Burke's extravagant reign.

"We'll be the envy of every library in the Southwest," Harrison said. He took the Porter print from Claire and balanced it between his long white fingers. Harrison had the hands of a pianist, but Claire doubted he played; his movements were stiff and unmusical, and his right hand always seemed to be out of synch with the left. "Now, tell me again why we want to have a Porter exhibit?"

Claire was tempted to say, "Because it will make us the envy of every other library in the Southwest," but she checked herself. "The library is very lucky to have these photos. They're much too beautiful to keep in a drawer."

Harrison fingered the photo. "But is there any historical significance?"

"Wouldn't you have liked to have exhibited the Edward Curtis photographs when they were new?"

"The Curtis photos were a record of a dying time and culture."

"These are a record of a sensibility," she said. Possibly even a dying sensibility, she thought.

Acquiring Burke's collection had put Harrison in an expansive mood, particularly since no library money had been spent. "All right," he said. "Go ahead with the exhibit."

"Thank you," Claire replied. "I'll arrange for someone in the mail room to bring in the books."

Harrison looked at his watch, more for effect than for information, Claire thought. She suspected that Harrison always knew exactly what time it was. "It's too late," he said. "They've gone home."

Harrison was the only one at the center who had windows in his office. They were set high in the wall near the ceiling. Claire looked up and saw evening rubbing its back against the glass. "I'll see if

Ralph can help me," she said. Harrison had the opportunity to offer his assistance, but he didn't take advantage of it.

Claire stopped at Ralph's office and found him hunched over his computer. When she asked him to help, he said he'd be glad to. Claire's hand truck was in the pickup. They took another from the storage room and wheeled it behind the library to the parking lot. The weather had turned cold, and the wind was gusty. Dark clouds scooted across the sky. The few people who were out walked quickly with their collars turned up against the wind. Claire told Ralph about Burke's collection while they walked.

"There's a *Banditti of the Plains*," she said. "The 1894 edition."

"I've never seen that book in the original edition," Ralph replied.

"Few people have. It puts the cattlemen of Wyoming in a bad light, and they went to great lengths to suppress it. What they couldn't buy up, they stole. They even hired an itinerant preacher to go into people's homes looking for copies. The book is subtitled 'The Cattleman's Invasion of Wyoming in 1892, The Crowning Infamy of the Ages.'"

"Crowning Infamy? That might be an overstatement, but they hung Cattle Kate, Queen of the Sweetwater, for taking stolen cattle in payment for her favors. She's one of my favorite Western women," Ralph said.

Claire laughed. She was partial to Cattle Kate, too, and to all the wild, defiant women of the Old West. They had reached the parking lot, which was badly in need of some overhead lights. Claire never liked coming here alone at night. As they walked toward her vehicle, Ralph continued talking about other Western women he admired, and Claire saw the damage before he did. The window on the passenger's side of her truck had been smashed, and the broken glass lay in pieces on the ground. Claire felt as if she'd been punched in the stomach. She remembered seeing the movie of Kipling's *Kim* as a child and watching an Indian fakir make glass shatter and come together again. She had the sensation that if she stared at the glass intensely enough, she could make the window whole and bring back whatever had been stolen from her truck.

Ralph continued talking about hookers and cowgirls, waiting for

Claire to take out her keys and open the door. "Oh, no," he said when he stopped and saw the damage. "What did they take? Your radio?"

"I hope that's all," Claire said.

Ralph circled the back of the truck. Claire looked into the window and saw what she feared most—an empty space on the passenger seat where the box of special books had been.

"The camper shell is intact," Ralph said.

"The radio is still here, but the special box of Burke's books is gone."

"Do you think they knew what they were getting?"

"Hard to say. I labeled that box valuable. Would you mind watching the truck for me while I go to my office and call university police?"

"Sure," Ralph said.

Claire paced the small space in front of her desk while she waited for the university police to show up. Rachel Dunbar, the policewoman who answered the call, came dressed in a tight-fitting uniform that was not designed for the female body. In a dress, Rachel might appear svelte, but the pants of her uniform stretched tight across her hips made her look lumpy as a pillow. Rachel had a wide face, bright eyes, unruly blonde hair, and an enthusiasm that led Claire to place her in her mid-twenties.

At the center, the librarians' offices all had glass walls, and it would be no secret to anyone walking by that Security was talking to Claire.

"You reported a theft?" Rachel said.

"Yes."

"Tell me about it."

"Have a seat." Claire motioned to the chair in front of her desk, but she was too tense to sit down herself. "I came back from Arizona today with Burke Lovell's book collection in my truck." Burke's name didn't cause a ripple in Rachel's calm face. "I put some of the more interesting and expensive books in a separate box. I took it into my motel room for safe keeping last night and put

40

it back on the front seat of my truck. All the other books were locked in the camper shell. I left the books in the truck while I came inside for a meeting. When I went back out to get them, the cab had been broken into and the box of special books had been stolen."

"I inspected the truck on my way over," Rachel said. "The window was smashed with a rock, and the door unlocked through the broken window. They didn't take your radio."

"I know."

"It might have been a casual thief. Someone who just passed by and saw an opportunity. A person walking through the university with a box of books isn't going to attract attention."

"I should have had the truck unloaded the minute I got here," Claire said. "I didn't think . . ."

"No one does, do they?" Rachel answered. "This is a university. The one place in Albuquerque we ought to feel safe."

Claire didn't expect the Albuquerque Police Department, who dealt with murder, rape, and child abuse every day, to pay attention to a box of books, but she hoped the university police would take the theft seriously. The expression on Rachel's face indicated she might.

"Can you put a value on the books?" she asked.

"I'd say somewhere around fifty thousand dollars."

"Whew! That's a lot. What was in there?"

"Some limited editions, some signed first editions. Willa Cather, Tony Hillerman, Edward Abbey. A folio of Ansel Adams photographs."

"I like Tony Hillerman," Rachel said.

Good, Claire thought. Maybe that will encourage her to get the books back.

"Did anybody else know what was in the box?" Rachel focused her sharp eyes on Claire.

"My coworkers knew."

"Did any of them have a grudge against you?"

"Not enough of a grudge to steal the books, I would hope."

"Library thefts are often inside jobs. Employees have the means and opportunity. As for motive, we all know about university salaries. I see the kinds of cars your coworkers drive."

"And what kind of car do you drive?" Claire asked.

"A Mustang."

Probably spends most of her paycheck on the payments, Claire thought.

"Your coworkers park in that lot. It would have been easy to put the books in a nearby car and drive away."

"The books are valuable, but they won't be easy to sell; some of them have fingerprint inscriptions, which are easy to identify. It's a limited market, and I know most of the people in it." Claire hated to think that the thief was a coworker. "Aren't there other motives for stealing?"

"Sure. There are kleptomaniacs who can't help themselves, people who steal for their own personal use, people who steal in anger to get back at somebody else. Addicts who steal because they need the money for a fix."

Claire saw Ruth O'Connor walk by the glass wall. Ruth stopped, stared at Rachel, and held an imaginary receiver to her ear indicating she expected a phone call the minute the policewoman left.

"Did anybody beside your coworkers know what was in the box?" Rachel asked.

"The Lovell family knew I was taking Burke's books; he donated them to the center."

"And how did they feel about that?"

"They weren't thinking about books when I saw them last; they were in shock. He died Saturday night."

"Where did he live?"

"In the Blue near Reserve."

"That's a long way to come to steal a box of books."

"True. And if the family wanted any of those books, all they had to do was ask."

"Could there have been something else in the box somebody wanted?"

"Such as?"

"Valuable papers, jewelry, electronics, cash. Those are the things that get stolen most often here."

"I had a copy of Burke's will, but I didn't put it in the box. It's in my purse."

"Is it a will some people are going to object to?"

"Probably."

"Are there any other copies?" When Rachel zeroed in on a question, her face lost its placidity and a strong underlying bone structure came into focus.

"There's one at the ranch."

"That's it?"

"I believe so."

"I'd make another copy if I were you, and put it someplace safe. Who was this Burke Lovell?"

"He was the director of the Center for Southwest Research for many years and a legend in the world of Western Americana."

"Must have been before my time."

"Must have been."

"But that doesn't mean I don't care about getting his books back." Rachel's eyes were bright with an investigator's zeal. There was a lot to be said for being young and new at the job, Claire thought.

"Good," Claire replied. "They mean a lot to me and to the library."

"There's a way librarians can put out word on the Internet that books were stolen isn't there?"

"Yes, but I don't know if Harrison will agree to it. The library doesn't like to advertise its thefts."

"That attitude makes our work harder."

"I know."

"I'll see what I can come up with in the way of physical evidence. With your help, we have a good chance of getting these books back."

"I hope you're right," said Claire.

"Can you give me an inventory?"

"Yes."

Rachel looked at the books and the artifacts on Claire's shelves.

"It's a big responsibility you librarians have taking care of all this stuff."

"We're the keepers of memory," Claire said.

As soon as Rachel left, Claire made two copies of Burke's will. She put the original back in her purse and locked the copies in her desk drawer. Then she reached for the phone to call Ruth O'Connor; but before she could dial the extension, Ruth poked her head in the door.

"What was *that* all about?" she asked.

"The box of Burke's most interesting and valuable books was stolen from my truck."

"And that young woman is investigating the theft?" Ruth's musical voice was full of innuendo.

"It could work to our advantage. She's enthusiastic about her job. She hasn't seen enough book thefts yet to become jaded."

"I don't have a very high opinion of university police; they seem to be more interested in stolen hubcaps than they are in books." She looked around her. "In their opinion, we already have more than enough books. When I reported the theft of some photographic plates a few years ago, a policeman told me he didn't know we kept china here. They might be impressed by the fact that a *Taos Pueblo* would sell for at least thirty thousand dollars."

"But who would buy it, Ruth? I intend to notify dealers, museums, and other libraries that it was stolen."

"Oh, there's always some unscrupulous person out there willing to pay the price."

"You could be right." Claire sighed.

"Maybe the thief doesn't intend to sell, maybe he just wants to add the books to his private collection."

"Or hers."

"Whatever," Ruth shrugged.

"In that case, we'll never get them back." The thought of the books ending up in the hands of a rogue collector was bad enough, but even worse was the thought that whoever took them wouldn't know their value and the books would end up moldering somewhere in a dump. When you have something valuable, you have the responsibility to take care of it. Claire felt she had failed. Her shoulders slumped, and her mood was turning dark.

Ruth fluttered around the tiny space in front of Claire's desk looking for ways to cheer her up. "You've had a bad weekend, haven't you? First you lose your mentor, then you lose some of his favorite books. Middle age is not for sissies."

"True." Claire knew Ruth was trying to make her laugh, but she didn't feel up to it.

Ruth escalated her efforts. She'd spent a year cheering up a sick husband and had some practice. "You know the books most often stolen from public libraries are *The Joy of Sex,* G.E.D. Exam books, and *The Prophecies of Nostradamus,* which means that the average thief is a high school dropout who has great sex and can foresee the future."

Claire had heard it before but she smiled, encouraging Ruth to continue. "In the Middle Ages the scribes put anathemas in their books to discourage vandals and thieves," Ruth said. "Maybe we should do that here. 'Who folds a leafe down, the devil toaste browne; Who makes marke or blotte, the devil toast hot; Who stealeth thisse book, the devil shall cooke.'"

This time Claire did laugh. She and Ruth went outside and helped Ralph and the university police bring the rest of the books in and stash them in the tower. When Rachel Dunbar was done examining her truck, Claire drove it home feeling a cold wind blowing through the broken window.

CHAPTER FOUR

Claire lived in the High Desert subdivision, a half hour drive from the university. In Tucson, Evan (who hated to drive) had insisted on living near the U of A in a subdivision where the houses were all white stucco with tile roofs that resembled flowerpots broken in half. In Tucson, the mountains remained in the distance silhouetted against the pale sky. In Albuquerque, Claire lived in the foothills and could observe the mountains up close in all their phases. At night they reflected the moon, and every piñon cast a shadow; in the morning they were a black outline against the rising sun; in midday a herd of resting gray elephants; in the evening, after the sun sank over the West Mesa, they turned the effervescent pink of sangria. Claire had been on the mountain once in the afterglow and felt she was immersed in sparkling wine. Her house had a small, walled yard xeriscaped with yucca and prickly pear by the previous owner, except for a rose garden along the east-facing wall. It had been too hot in Tucson to grow roses; they soaked up water like an insatiable sponge. Claire knew in spring she'd be battling aphids, but she'd also get to see the color of the buds.

When she got home, Nemesis rubbed against her legs to welcome her back. She changed the litter and filled his dish. He wanted to go out, but that was forbidden after dark when coyotes took control of her yard and Nemesis's white fur and house cat smell made him an easy target. The neighborhood seemed tame enough by day, but at night it belonged to the predators. The closer one lived to the foothills, the more pets got taken. Claire could hear the coyotes at night barking and singing. As long as she knew Nemesis was inside, the sound was thrilling.

Evening was the time when she felt most divorced—no one to talk to, no one to cook dinner for but herself. She boiled water, threw in some frozen tortellini and a handful of frozen peas. Evan had insisted on a real meal every night plus a salad. Frozen tortellini did not satisfy his needs. To give him credit, he did the dishes and he talked during dinner mostly about himself and his work. Evan was an anthropologist at the U of A, superficially quiet and intellectual, but there was something deep and unyielding about him. Claire had spent twenty-eight years circling his unreasonable core. Evan was a spring wound too tight. In middle age the spring came unwound, and he got involved with a graduate student.

Claire wondered whether the new wife, Melissa, cooked dinner every night. Evan had a chance to remake himself and not have a salad every damn day of the week, but she doubted he'd take it. Melissa was thirty-eight years old, a perpetual graduate student, blonde, fit, and deeply in debt. She eked out a living taking people on archaeology tours while she pursued her Ph.D. on student loans. It was obvious what Evan saw in her, but Claire had to wonder what she saw in him. She knew his every flaw and wrinkle. She knew how annoyingly predictable, inconsiderate, and demanding he could be. In the heat of anger after finding out about Melissa, Claire had offered to write her a letter thanking her for ending the marriage. "Our marriage ended years ago" was Evan's pompous reply.

Claire hadn't written the letter, but she kept track of all the ways she was glad to be rid of Evan, calling them her "Poor Melissa" moments. For example, she could eat what she wanted to eat when she wanted to eat it without an argument. But just as she sat down to her Poor Melissa tortellini, the phone rang. It was the time of day when Anonymous and Unavailable were out trolling for suckers, so Claire waited to see what appeared on her call screening box before picking up. She saw a New Mexico number she didn't recall, but the name under it, Burke P. Lovell, gave her a chill.

"Hello," she answered tentatively.

"Claire?"

"Yes."

"It's Corinne."

"How are you doing, Corinne?"

"Getting by."

"Did Samantha arrive?"

"Yes. She was here. The reason I'm calling is we wanted to let you and the other people at the library know that we are having a service here Saturday. We're going to bury my father on the ranch. Everyone's pretty distraught, so we decided to keep it to just the neighbors and the family. I hope the people at the library will understand."

"I'm sure they will. We intend to have a memorial service for him here, although I don't know when yet. I hope you can come."

"It's a long way," sighed Corinne.

Two hundred and twenty miles, thought Claire, far enough to make it possible to bring up the subject of the will but not the theft of the books. "Corinne, I think you should know that Burke made me his personal representative in his will. I'll be in charge of settling the estate."

"Oh, we know that," Corinne replied. "Kass told us and showed us the will after you left." The line was picking up static somewhere in the long distance between Albuquerque and the Blue.

"I'll need to come out there to go through his papers."

"Okay. Just tell me when," Corinne said, hanging up.

Claire went back to her tortellini, but it had gotten cold and soggy. She dumped it in the disposal, ground it into mush, and made herself a bowl of microwave popcorn. When she finished the popcorn, she decided to take a hot bath and go to bed. She ran the water in the tub, poured in a pine-scented bath oil, lit a candle, and slid in. This was the time she had reserved to cry about Burke. Claire didn't find it easy to cry, and since she'd taken the scissors to her own life and gotten divorced, it had become even harder. She sat in the tub for an hour remembering Burke, letting the tears come.

She spent a restless night and woke before dawn, but lay in bed waiting for the sun to rise and crack the sky behind the mountains.

She got up then and started the day with the infinite ultimate stance moving on through felling a tree, leopard punch, repulse monkey, and ending by embracing the tiger. Ordinarily her movements were slow, graceful, and yin, but this morning they were fast, forceful, and yang. Tai chi was an elegant dance capable of keeping old ladies tranquil and limber, but Claire didn't intend to become a tranquil old lady; she thought the women who did best remained fierce. Tai chi was a meditation, but tai chi chuan was a martial art, a way of throwing an opponent off balance and causing the opponent's defeat. Claire grew up with an athletic older brother; the fights they had were physical, and combat didn't necessarily intimidate her. She started practicing tai chi chuan during the bad days of the divorce, and the martial aspect helped her to fend off her anger and keep her balance. This morning she imagined she was defending herself against a thief. Since the attacker was unknown and amorphous (yin), she had to be firm (yang), whereas if an opponent mounted an aggressive attack, the victim could be yielding. In tai chi chuan every action embraced its opposite. Warriors won because they knew their opponents better than their opponents knew them. Claire's objective was to know the thief and to draw that person out of hiding.

When she finished embracing the tiger, she showered, got dressed, and called her friend Madelyn in Tucson, hoping to catch her before she left for her job at the U of A. Claire intended to tell Madelyn about Burke's death, but Madelyn already knew. "It must be hard for you," she said. "First you lose your father, then your husband, now your mentor. All those strong male images gone from your life."

"I've been embracing the tiger," Claire said.

Madelyn laughed. She had introduced Claire to tai chi chuan and had encouraged her to get the divorce. Madelyn was several years younger than Claire and remained resolutely single, espousing Katherine Hepburn's philosophy: Why exchange the admiration of many for the criticism of one? She was good-looking enough—with thick auburn hair and a lush body—to get away with it.

"I feel terrible about Burke," Claire told her.

"Kind of a weird way to die, don't you think? Outside in the snow?"

"I think it was what he wanted."

"The daughter took the blanket off him?"

"Apparently."

"That's familial love?"

"It might be tough love."

"I thought Burke only had two daughters."

"So did he until Mariah tracked him down, the product of one of his liaisons, I guess."

"Well, there were plenty of those when he worked here. I assume he slowed down in recent years. What do you hear about the funeral?"

"The family is having a private service at the ranch."

"And who gets the book collection?"

"We do."

"Ah." Madelyn sighed, and Claire could see her doing it. Madelyn had a taste for drama and wore bright red lipstick that framed her sighs and exclamations. "Lucky you!"

"Not so lucky as it turns out. I set aside some of the books I thought special, and the box was stolen from my truck in the university parking lot."

"What was in the box?"

Claire told her.

"We have most of those books in the library, including the Austin/Adams folio and deWitt's *History of the Blue*. Why did you put that book in your special box? It's not exactly collectible."

"It was mis-shelved, and I set it aside. When I got done packing, there was room in that box."

"The one book you mentioned I know we don't have but wish we did is *The Brave Cowboy*. The print run was minuscule, and the people who bought it read it to pieces. It was published before Abbey became a god. That's the book you ought to be searching for. *Taos Pueblo* is likely to get broken, and the photos ripped out and sold individually. *The Brave Cowboy* will be in demand, especially now that Abbey's dead and there'll be no new work. That's a book dealers will be very reluctant to give up. What is more important to you, getting the books back or catching the thief?"

"If I had to choose, I'd say the books, but it would be nice to find out who took them. If we knew who, that could lead us to the books."

"If the thief doesn't get rid of them or trash them first. If we have the opportunity to buy the books, should we do it? I know Harrison got the job because he's tighter than a tick. Can you find a way to reimburse us?"

The gentlemen's code in the rare book world said that a dealer or librarian who unknowingly buys a stolen book takes the loss and returns the book to its owner. But someone who knowingly buys a stolen book couldn't be expected to do that. "I'll find a way to pay you back," Claire said.

"The best solution would be for us to go ahead and buy them, and get as much information as possible about the seller. But you realize that the odds are we'll never see those books. They're far more likely to go to some unscrupulous collector."

"I know, but thanks for your help."

"Glad to do it," Madelyn said. "Let me know how it turns out."

"I will."

Claire dropped the truck off at the Chevy dealer to get the broken window fixed, and got a ride to work in a courtesy van. The driver let her off at the university bookstore on Central, and she walked across the campus. The woman in the Jimenez sculpture danced seductively and flipped her skirt. The vendors on the plaza sold hand-knit sweaters from Peru and embroidered vests from Guatemala. Students hurried to class, lugging backpacks full of books. Claire couldn't help wondering if any of those backpacks contained Burke Lovell's books.

Zimmerman Library, where the Center for Southwest Research was located, had been designed by the architect John Gaw Meem. The main part of the building was massive and thick and grounded in the earth, but the tower beside it reached for the sky and was the university's signature building. Zimmerman had a tower and it had tunnels, aspirations and secrets that fueled Claire's imagination.

Her first order of business was Harrison Hough, who was likely to have heard about the theft by now. When she entered his office, he sat at his desk with the overhead light beaming down on his head. While they talked, he turned a paper clip over and over in his long, pianist's fingers. Harrison collected folk art. A papier-mâché Day of the Dead skeleton sat in death's cart and grinned at her from the shelf behind his desk.

"Did the thief get the Austin/Adams folio?" he asked.

"I'm afraid so."

"At least the history books are safe." Claire suspected that her taste for fiction marked her as an unreliable romantic in Harrison's eyes.

"They've been stored in the tower." Where Claire hoped they would remain safe. Zimmerman had been robbed before. There was a better security system now, but no system was foolproof against someone who wanted to break in badly enough.

"Why didn't you bring in the books immediately?" Harrison scowled, and shadows settled into his frown lines emphasizing the severity of his expression. The admiration of yesterday had turned to disapprobation today.

"I wanted to get to the meeting on time. I'd like to try to get the stolen books back."

"How do you intend to do that?" Harrison unfolded the paper clip, dropped it, and picked up another.

"By contacting other libraries and book dealers, any place the thief might try to sell them."

"Be discreet. We don't want the state to think we can't protect their assets."

"I'd like to put them on BamBam." It was the Web site where librarians listed stolen books.

Harrison shook his head. "Not a good idea."

Claire knew what he was thinking. A listing on the Internet was a way of announcing to state officials and potential thieves that security was poor at Zimmerman and books were ripe for the taking.

On the other hand, the more people who knew about the theft, the better the chances were for getting the books back. But Claire didn't expect to change Harrison's mind.

"All right," she said.

On the way to her office she stopped at the kitchen to get a cup of coffee. Gail Benton stood at the sink looking out the window and gulping down a large white pill with a glass of water. She didn't hear Claire enter. Gail looked more disheveled than usual this morning in a baggy gray sweater and a skirt with a drooping hemline. Sometimes when she came upon Gail unexpectedly, the expression in her eyes was raw and jealous, a look Claire's children called the stink eye. This look of naked competition always startled her, although she saw it often enough in academia. It was disturbing to Claire that someone could want her job so badly, but ridiculous at the same time. It was said about academics that the competition was so brutal because the stakes were so small: a title, an office, a salary the size of a secretary's. What they were really competing for, Claire thought, was the love of an indifferent parent. If Harrison was a surrogate daddy, Gail ought to be very pleased with herself because Claire was on his shit list now.

"Good morning, Gail," she said.

Gail turned away from the window. "Claire! I didn't hear you coming." She dropped the glass she'd been holding into the sink. It was plastic, and although it bounced, it didn't break. "What a shame about Burke's books!" Her sympathetic words were at odds with her sour expression.

"It is," Claire replied.

"I hope they come back to the library."

"So do I."

Claire poured herself a cup of coffee and went back to her office, where she typed up an inventory of the missing books for Rachel. She e-mailed the list to the out-of-print booksellers, museum administrators, and university librarians she knew across the Southwest. The books were most likely to surface in the Southwest; it was where they'd command the best price. If she didn't know the e-mail address, Claire called. Book dealers were usually civilized people, and she expected their cooperation. Everyone she talked to was sorry about Burke, everyone agreed to help.

After she'd contacted everybody she could think of, she went to BookFinder.com to search all the Web sites, where out-of-print books were bought and sold even though she didn't expect the books to surface so soon. And she didn't expect the Taos folio to surface on the Internet at any time; it was too rare, too valuable, too easy to trace. There were hundreds of Hillermans for sale, so many that Claire wondered if there weren't more sellers out there than buyers. Some of the books, she knew, were ghosts in the system—books that were already sold but hadn't been deleted yet. One effect of Internet sales could be to flood the market and depress prices. It used to take initiative to track down a rare book, but now it could be done with a click of the keys. When Claire searched for a first edition of *The Brave Cowboy,* however, she didn't find a single copy. The only *Brave Cowboy* available was in a limited edition that had been signed by Kirk Douglas, who starred in the movie.

She logged out of BookFinder, took out her Abbey bibliography, and checked *Black Sun* against it. She'd been right; the pub date was May of 1971. But she would have taken more pleasure in being right if she could have gone down the hall and told Burke so. "God damn it, Claire," he would have said. "I expect you to be right."

Remembering her promise to Sheriff Henner, she put a copy of Burke's will in an envelope and addressed it to him in Reserve.

CHAPTER FIVE

On Thursday Claire drove across town to keep her appointment with the lawyer, Sally Froelich. Downtown Albuquerque was canyon country, full of the shadows cast by hotels and office buildings but void of people. Only the homeless spent any time on the street. Everyone else conducted his or her business and hurried back to their offices and cars. Sally Froelich's office was a few blocks from downtown in a small, well-maintained Victorian house with burglar bars on the windows. One of Claire's criteria when shopping for a house in Albuquerque was that it didn't have bars on the windows, which meant living deep in the valley or high in the Heights, nowhere near the middle of town.

Sally was a solo practitioner specializing in wills, trusts, estates, and probate, and a woman of generous proportions. The lavender cotton dress she wore emphasized her size, leading Claire to assume she was comfortable with it. Sally had thick brown hair that hung down her back. Her face was as wrinkled as an unmade bed. Her brown eyes were large and warm. She wore a silver ear cuff wrapped around the side of one ear. Claire was relieved she wouldn't be working with a tense, buttoned-down lawyer in a boring suit. The room Sally worked in was as comfortable as a home office. The curtains on the windows concealed the burglar bars. There was a thick carpet on the floor. A painting from the Taos school hung on the wall. Sally's polished desk was lit by a lamp with a green glass shade. The desktop was empty except for a silver letter opener and cup that held pencils and pens. The room, an island of tradition and stability, made it easy to forget downtown Albuquerque was on the other side of the window and that homeless people were pushing their shopping carts down the street.

Sally offered tea and served it in a china cup. Claire settled into a wing chair, sipping the tea. "You have beautiful things," she said.

"My business is stiffs and gifts." Sally laughed.

"It may seem genteel and cozy in here, but probate can be a nasty business. Sometimes it's just as nasty as criminal law."

"I don't doubt it." Claire put her cup and saucer down on the polished desk. "Is this an antique?"

Sally nodded. "It belonged to my grandfather and my father. They were both lawyers in Hillsboro."

Hillsboro was one of the New Mexican villages that Claire loved. "What brought you to Albuquerque?

"Opportunity. Adventure."

Motives that Claire understood. "Ruth O'Connor referred me to you."

"How is she doing?"

"Far better than anyone expected."

"It's good that Robert went first. He would have been lost without her, but the widows usually find a way to cope." Sally put her arms on the desk and looked Claire in the eye. "What can I do for you?"

"An old friend of mine died recently and made me the personal representative in his will. Here's a copy. I don't know what a personal representative does, and Ruth thought you could help."

"It can be quite a responsibility in New Mexico, particularly if the assets are substantial."

"They are."

"First of all you are required to give notice of your appointment to the heirs and the devisees. The heirs are the people entitled to receive property under the laws of intestate succession, and the devisees are the people designated in the will to receive property."

"I think the devisees already know."

"Even so, you should put it in writing. You will need to prepare an inventory and an appraisal of the decedent's property, to take control of the estate, to give notice to creditors, and to pay claims allowed against the estate. Is there any question of who the heirs are?"

"There could be."

"I'd suggest hiring a genealogical search company to locate all of them. I can recommend Brown's Genealogical Service in Denver. Here's the number."

"Thanks."

Sally held the will in her hand. "I'll take a look at this, and in the meantime why don't you get the letters out to the devisees."

"All right," Claire answered.

"I'll bill the estate hourly for my time." Sally stood up, signaling that the meeting was over. "I'm looking forward to working with you," she said, shaking Claire's hand.

"Me, too," Claire replied. She thought Sally would be pleasant to work with and the office was charming, but she hoped she wouldn't be spending too much time here. It was obvious she would have to spend time in the Blue, and she had mixed feelings about that. She loved the ranch, but it wouldn't be the same without Burke.

After dinner that night Claire got on her PC and played a couple of hands of computer solitaire. She liked the odds in solitaire; she won often enough to make it rewarding, lost often enough to keep it interesting. She played until she had an easy win, then she typed the letters to Samantha, James, Corinne, and Mariah, notifying them that she was Burke Lovell's personal representative.

The following Tuesday she got a call telling her that Samantha Lovell was at the information desk. Claire had been expecting a reaction from Samantha, but not this reaction. She walked out to the information desk, trying to remember how long it had been since she'd seen Samantha. Several years at least. At a distance she didn't look a day older—still slender and blonde—but up close Claire could see fine lines radiating from the corners of her eyes. The New Mexico sun could be unforgiving, but it warmed even the coldest days. When people went out, they dressed for the temperature in their car not the temperature outside. Samantha, in New Mexico style, wore no jacket. She did wear a lot of silver and turquoise Indian jewelry over a black dress. Her blonde hair was held up in a clip and carefully tousled.

Samantha gave her a hug, kissed the air in the vicinity of her cheek, and said, "Nice to see you," in a voice that was a thin layer of ice over a freezing cold river.

"You, too," Claire replied, trying to put some warmth in her own voice.

"Can we talk?"

"Let's go to the Garden Court and get something to drink." Claire didn't want to air grievances about the will in her glass cage of an office.

They walked to the Garden Court in silence, picked up coffee in the cafeteria line, and sat down at a table in the window looking down on the campus.

"I'm very sorry about your father," Claire began. "I know what it's like to lose a parent."

"Do you?"

"My father died last year."

"I got your letter." Samantha ignored her coffee and studied Claire with hard eyes. "I always liked you, Claire. I cannot believe you are participating in this fraud."

"There's no fraud, Samantha. Your father asked me to be his personal representative. I'm following his wishes. That's all."

"He was on Valium and Jack Daniel's. He didn't know what he was doing when he signed that will."

"The will was made out beforehand. He'd had time to think about it. I understand why you're not happy with the terms, but he seemed perfectly sober and rational to me when he signed it. I think the nurse and Jed will attest to that."

"Doesn't it seem suspicious to you that as soon as the will is signed, the primary heir, Mariah, takes my father outside and arranges for him to die?"

Claire aligned her back against her chair. "I don't know that Ma-

58

riah was aware the will was signed that afternoon, and it appears that Burke chose his own death."

"If he took his own life, then why didn't he leave us a suicide note?"

The will was his note, Claire thought, but she kept the thought to herself. Samantha wrapped her hands around her mug, and Claire noticed that she was wearing long, polished, artificial nails, and every finger had a silver ring.

"We're asking the Catron County DA to investigate, to do an autopsy and a drug screening," Samantha said. "Assisted suicide is a crime in New Mexico." A muscle near her cheekbone twitched as if a cricket had crawled under her skin.

Claire wondered what would happen to the terms of the will if Mariah was prosecuted for Burke's death. It certainly would make it easier for the family to gain control of the ranch.

"Mariah shows up out of nowhere, claiming to be my father's daughter, and you believe that?"

"Apparently he believed it. That's what matters, isn't it?"

"I suggested she take a DNA test to prove her claim, but she refused."

"Maybe she resented being asked." Claire expected the truth of Mariah's claim to be proven or disproven by the genealogical search, but she didn't want to get into that with Samantha yet.

"She's a member of a radical environmentalist group. We believe Mariah's a front for them and that they are scheming to gain control of the ranch and do us out of our inheritance."

"I understand how difficult this is for you, Samantha, but it was your father's stated wish that the ranch go to Mariah to be used for a wildlife preserve. When I agreed to be his personal representative I agreed to uphold his wishes. You are being provided for."

"With what? Two hundred thousand dollars?"

Claire knew that two hundred thousand dollars would barely buy a starter home in Santa Fe. She wondered how Samantha was earning her living. "What are you doing now?" she asked.

"Working as a massage therapist."

It was one of those low-paying jobs that people gravitate to in

Santa Fe, where professional jobs are hard to find. In some ways Samantha reminded Claire of Evan's new wife, Melissa. Both were tall, slender blondes with little ability to earn money and a lot of ability to attract men. "You know that your father left his book collection to the center?"

"Yes."

"Is there anything you'd like? I made that offer to James, and I'd like to do the same for you and Mariah and Corinne."

Samantha stared out the window at the students walking by. "I'll think about it."

"A box of the books was stolen from my truck after I got back here." Claire waited for a reaction, but she didn't get one.

Samantha turned the conversation to personal matters. "I hear you got divorced."

Claire had been more comfortable talking about books. "Yes."

"You were married for a long time."

"Twenty-eight years."

"Anybody new in your life?"

"No. I like being on my own. And you?" Claire expected there to be someone, possibly someone richer and older.

"I've been seeing an artist named Rusty Siler."

Claire had never heard of him, but she thought it might be considered rude to say so. "Is he with a gallery?"

"Not yet," Samantha answered with a defensive tone that made Claire suspect Rusty wasn't a very successful artist. Samantha struck her as a woman who had been deeply bruised as a child and who seemed to go through life pressing the wound over and over again. No amount of money or beauty or men would change that. Claire felt her job would be a lot easier if only Burke had paid more attention to his children. The world would be easier if everyone had paid more attention to their children. "I want you to know that we've hired a lawyer. His name is Walter Massey, and he will be getting in touch with you. We're considering contesting the will."

"On what grounds?"

"That my father was not of sound mind when he signed it. That Mariah is not who she claims to be."

"It's your choice." Claire's voice was calm, but she could feel heat rising and flushing her face.

When they finished their coffee, Claire walked Samantha back to her car, which she'd parked in the visitor's lot next to the university bookstore. It was dusted with a layer of brown dirt that made it impossible to tell how old the vehicle was or what condition it was in, but Claire could tell it was one of those big, tippy SUV's that gets terrible gas mileage, rolls easily in an accident, and does a lot of damage when it plows into a smaller car.

When she got back to her office, Claire called Sally Froelich. She expected that one day now, the face of the person she called would appear on her computer screen, replacing the books with wings that were her screen saver. Whenever Claire's computer was idle for ten minutes, the classics leaped off their shelves and flew across her screen. For now she'd have to settle for a mental image of the person at the other end of the line. She saw Sally as sitting at her polished desk surrounded by beautiful things.

"Samantha Lovell, Burke's daughter, came to see me today," Claire began.

"Oh?" said Sally. Claire imagined her eyebrows plowing furrows in her forehead.

"She's not happy with the terms of the will."

"I'm not surprised now that I've read it. The will certainly favors daughter Mariah. Is she the one who cared for Burke in his old age? Often that's the child the parent remembers with gratitude."

"I think it's more likely she charmed him. There was a private nurse, and Corinne, Burke's oldest daughter, lived at the ranch. Burke was well taken care of. Mariah has an adorable child, Burke's only grandson, and she shares his interest in turning the ranch into a nature preserve. He feared if the other children got the property, they would sell it.

"Would they?"

"They might. James lives in Phoenix, and Samantha lives in Santa Fe. They weren't close to Burke, and they're not interested in the ranch. I imagine Corinne could be swayed by them. Burke wasn't a particularly good parent."

"How come Mariah turned out all right? Assuming she did turn out all right."

"Burke had nothing to do with her upbringing. They only discovered each other recently."

"Oh," said Sally. "Well the deceased's parenting skills aren't the issue here. Your job is to see that his wishes are carried out."

"That's why I'm calling. Samantha told me the family has hired a lawyer, and they're considering contesting the will."

"Whom did they hire? Did she say?"

"Walter Massey."

"That bag of wind," Sally snorted. "On what grounds do they intend to contest?"

"That Burke was under the influence when he signed the will and not of sound mind."

"Is that true?"

"I was there, and he seemed perfectly rational to me. The witnesses can corroborate that. He did have a drink at dinner, and apparently he took some Valium later that night. The family asked the DA to do an autopsy and are waiting for the results of a drug test."

"That won't establish exactly when he ingested the drugs, so your testimony and that of the witnesses will be important. I noticed he bequeathed his book collection to UNM. Do you stand to benefit from that?"

"Not financially, but it will help my career. A box of books that I set aside was stolen from my car after I got back to the library. I'm trying to find a way to get them back. Would there be any money from the estate if I have to pay for them?"

"I doubt it, since the books were in your hands when they were stolen. I'd check the library's insurance policy."

"Samantha also says the family is asking the Catron County DA to prosecute Mariah for assisted suicide."

Sally laughed. "I don't think that's going to happen. Law enforcement in Catron County gets hired by whether or not they fit the uniform. Assisting a suicide is a crime that's unlikely to get prosecuted there. They believe that if a man wants to kill himself, he can kill himself; although I suppose the method used is unusual. Out there they usually blow their brains out."

"Samantha says they don't believe Mariah is Burke's daughter, which could also be grounds for overturning the will."

"Is she?"

"She says she is. He said she was."

"It's typical of Massey to try every sleazy trick in the book and to run up a big fat fee. If he wins, the fees come out of the estate and all the devisees pay. If they lose, it comes out of the challengers' pockets or their inheritance. Massey will get paid no matter how frivolous the lawsuit. No matter who wins, he wins. I've seen cases like this where the whole estate goes to pay legal fees. The genealogical search should establish whether Mariah is the daughter, but that will take a few weeks. Did you call them?"

"Yes."

"I don't know that it will make any difference. I have the will in front of me, and it says Burke Lovell is leaving the ranch to Mariah Geraty, not to his daughter Mariah Geraty. Why does she use the name Geraty?"

"I don't know. It's her mother's name? A husband's name?"

"Something for you to find out. You've got your work cut out for you."

But Claire had her work cut out for her at the library, too.

"Are you planning on going over there anytime soon?"

"I'll have to."

"While you're there, take a copy of the will to Lovell's bank, and get permission to write checks on the account. You'll need to keep the estate's bills current. And see if you can find a copy of the deed. We'll need that, too. Keep track of your hours. You will be compensated for your time and expenses."

Claire wondered what would compensate her for her time away from the library.

After she got off the phone, Claire went to the Internet to see if any of the stolen books had been listed for sale yet. The Internet was the perfect place for a thief to operate, since no one needed to know the seller's name, age, sex, address, or even what country that person lived in. Claire wondered how the exchange of funds would take place, always a problem when doing business over the Internet. Did the seller trust the buyer to pay? Did the buyer trust the seller to deliver the books? Claire had heard that even cashier's checks could be forged. The way to sell books anonymously, she decided, would be COD through UPS or another shipper. The seller would use a phony name and insist on cash or a cashier's check made out to cash. Claire hoped her thief would not be smart enough to figure this out. She might be able to buy the books back, but she'd never find out who had stolen them. She wanted to know who; the books had been in her truck in her care. The theft felt like a personal attack.

First she went to Dejanews, the search engine for news groups. There were news groups for every interest Claire could imagine, and some she couldn't. Rec.arts.books was a place fans got online to compare notes about favorite books, as well as to buy and sell them. Professional booksellers tended to use Web sites such as Bibliofind or Alibris that charged a fee, but news groups were free, and amateurs bought and sold there. Claire searched for Tony Hillerman, and got two hundred and fifty hits. She opened all the messages dated after the day the books were stolen. Several *A Thief of Times* were for sale on the rec.arts.mystery news group, but none of them had been illustrated by Ernie Franklin. When she searched for *The Brave Cowboy,* she didn't get a single response. *A Thief of Time* had a first printing somewhere around two hundred thousand. *The Brave Cowboy* would have been closer to two thousand.

Claire got out of Dejanews, went to BookFinder.com, and searched for *The Brave Cowboy* again. She felt a tinge of excitement whenever she sent a query out into the wide world of cyber space, but her computer was having a slow day, and excitement turned to impatience while she waited for an answer. She drummed the desk with her fingers until *The Brave Cowboy* came up. This time, in addition to all the limited editions signed by Kirk Douglas, Alibris had a first edition, very fine, with no wrapper at a price of seven hundred dollars, the correct price for that book without an inscription or a dust jacket.

Claire knew Rex Barker, the dealer who had listed it. Rex was a dealer in Western Americana and modern firsts who operated on the fringes of the rare-book world. He was six feet three and skinny as a post. He liked to gamble, drank Jack Daniel's, and had once written a well-reviewed book of poetry. That was enough to set him apart in the rare-book business, but he also happened to be the only dealer who lived in Socorro, New Mexico, a town that was a blip beside the Interstate. Claire had always found Rex to be a shrewd dealer and very quick to spot a hot new writer. He was drawn to small print runs like a coyote to a coddled pet. Sometimes he bought up a publisher's entire stock of a book, storing them in his garage and parceling them out as sparingly as DeBeers' diamonds while he waited for the writer's reputation to grow and the price to escalate. Some people found this tactic offensive, but Claire felt the books were better off appreciating in Rex's garage than they were getting pulped. Rex liked to talk about how close he'd been to Edward Abbey. Hanging out with Edward Abbey resembled sleeping with John Kennedy. If all the people who claimed to actually had, neither man would have gotten any work done. Claire was surprised that Rex would sell an Abbey, but he could well be in a situation where he needed the money. It happened often enough in the rare-book world.

She had left a message on Rex's machine after the theft, and mailed him a list of the stolen books. She wondered if someone had sold Burke's *Brave Cowboy* to Rex and had taken off or damaged the jacket not knowing how valuable it was. She called and waited through his message, knowing that Rex screened his calls.

"Rex, this is Claire," she said. "Pick up if you're there. I want to talk to you about *The Brave Cowboy* you listed on Alibris."

He came on the line. "Hi. I had that book before Burke died. It's not his," he said quickly.

"Is there an inscription?"

"No."

"You should have had Abbey sign it before he died."

"If I'd had it then, I would have."

Claire had his word that he wasn't marketing the stolen Abbey. For some people that wouldn't be enough. Still, she knew Rex to be too shrewd a trader to sell an inscribed book at an uninscribed price. To test him, she offered to buy the book for the listed price of seven hundred dollars.

"Too late," he said. "I sold it this morning."

"Full price?" she asked.

"Full price." Rex wasn't much of a talker, and that was all he had to say.

When Claire got home that night she let Nemesis out and watched the sunset while he ran around the yard on the trail of a bird or a rodent. The best sunsets were in the winter when wood smoke and pollution turned the colors even more intense. When the sun dropped behind the West Mesa, it outlined the clouds near the horizon in gold. The color reflected off the clouds high in the sky, then slid up the Sandias, turning them the color of pink zinfandel. Nemesis's white fur began to stand out in the growing darkness. Claire called, and when he didn't respond, she lured him inside with a dish of tuna. She checked the call screening box (all the calls were from Anonymous and Unavailable), went into her study, and logged on to her PC. She had decided to put out a want list for some of the stolen books, and couldn't do that anonymously on unm.edu, the university's net server. Anyone outside the university would realize the request had come from within, and anyone inside would know it had come from her. Claire maintained an account on AOL so she could e-mail her children and friends in privacy. She'd followed AOL's advice of making her screen name a series of numbers, but it was hard to remember a string of meaningless numbers. Her own birth date would have been too obvious, so she used her mother's. She saw her coworkers often enough that she'd had no reason to give her screen name to them.

She figured there had to be a way to search a person's screen name on the Internet. Claire went to Netscape, clicked on e-mail finder, entered her own name, and got the message that no listings matched her search criteria. Either AOL had honored her request not to list her name or e-mail finder was not yet state of the art. Then she did a reverse lookup to see if searching her e-mail address would produce her name. Once she put out her request, a seller might search to see who her screen name belonged to, but the chances were good the seller wouldn't find her. Once again, she got the message that no listings matched her search criteria.

Claire couldn't list too many of the stolen books without alerting the thief. The scarcity of the limited edition of the Austin/Adams folio made it far too obvious. She decided to try *The Brave Cowboy;* it was hard to find, but first editions did show up every now and then. If Rex had been lying, he might respond to her query. Since she didn't know whether she was looking for an amateur or a professional, she put her query on Alibris, Bibliofind, and rec.arts. Her message read, "Collector seeking *The Brave Cowboy* by Edward Abbey, very fine, will pay top dollar." She decided to leave off the dust jacket as a way of testing Rex. She gave no phone number or snail mail address. The only way to respond would be by e-mail. Claire had set her trap. There was nothing to do but wait and see if anyone took the bait.

She preferred using AOL at night. Looking at the subject lines of her unsolicited messages in the morning could ruin the day, but the next morning she was eager to see if her query had gotten any response. She had fifteen messages, all of them trying to catch her eye with a subject line that was only a few words long. Six messages came from the hotmail list server. "Hi," said Tanya and Michelle. "Hot college stud," said Brad. Claire made it a point to automatically delete anything that came from hotmail. She had tried to block it, but the gods of cyber space had not favored her request. If biblio thieves were people who had great sex and liked Nostradamus's prophecies, then AOL users were people who had perverted cyber sex, a bad credit rating, and wanted to get rich setting up pyramid schemes from home.

The only subject line that interested Claire was two parentheses reversed and back-to-back that came from 876543@compuserve.

She opened that one and found the entire message was a smiling face composed of parentheses, dots, and dashes. It might be a spam mail wishing millions of people a nice day. It could have come from someone who'd seen *The Brave Cowboy* query and figured out it came from her. It could even have come from Rex Barker. It wasn't the e-mail address she had for him, but he might have more than one account or be using someone else's. It was easy to get paranoid when dealing on the Internet. Claire composed a frowning face with parentheses and dashes and a period for the nose, hit the send now button, and returned it to the sender.

CHAPTER SIX

On Friday morning Claire took the day off from the library and returned to the Blue. She needed to get there on a weekday to take care of the business at the bank. It was a cold morning, and ice clustered all over her windshield. Her breath hovered in front of her while she scraped off the ice. She drove across town on Paseo del Norte and saw smoke rising from chimneys in the valley as it might have risen from fires long before the conquistadors arrived. A heron-shaped cloud floated above the West Mesa. A flock of ravens lifted off a power line, rising and falling like notes on a musical score. On I-25 the road belonged to distracted commuters putting on makeup and talking on cell phones. On I-40 it belonged to truckers determined to make it to California. After she turned south on State Highway 117 an hour later, the road belonged to her. The highway set her mind wandering.

Claire had spent the summer after her sophomore year of college traveling around Europe. She started out with her girlfriends but ended up with Pietro, an Italian student she met in Spain. Her friends went back to France, but Claire and Pietro continued south in his VW van, having coffee in a café every morning, picking out a place on the map and going there. They took the ferry from Algeciras to Tangiers. From Tangiers they went south to Rabat, Casablanca, Fez, and Marrakesh, wandering through a maze of medinas. Many people saw a resemblance to Spain in the high plains of New

Mexico, but in the narrow, winding streets of the adobe pueblos, Claire could see Morocco, too. It intrigued her that the Spaniards had ended up in a place so similar to the one they'd left behind.

Traveling with Pietro, Claire discovered the pleasures of the lines between the dots on the map, that it was the going that mattered, not the destination. She didn't return to school until the spring semester. Pietro was the first romance of her life. She thought he would be the last, but they quarreled and separated in Venice, and three years later she was married to Evan, who never picked a place on a map and just went. When he traveled every stop was planned, every motel and restaurant recommended in the AAA guidebook, budgets were followed, mileage was calculated. When Evan got stuck in traffic, he swore and pounded the steering wheel. They argued over what to listen to on the radio. Evan liked talk shows and PBS. Claire liked music. Poor Melissa, Claire thought, inserting Vivaldi into her CD.

Having a job and doing it well was rewarding. Having a family and watching them grow and thrive had been deeply satisfying. But Claire had never forgotten the lure of the open road and a day with no agenda, and she still wondered what had become of Pietro, whether he'd gotten middle-aged, bald, and fat, whether he was even alive. In some ways, her life was an open highway again, with a yellow line curving in front of her. She thought little of driving a couple of hundred miles to see a friend. She'd gotten across the hormonal divide, and could have thirty or more healthy years to do whatever she wanted. Sometimes she felt the divorce had pushed her out of the nest with her wings still wet. It wasn't where she'd expected to be at this point in life, but it wasn't a bad place to be, either. She lived in a time when people had to reinvent themselves; jobs were lost, marriages dissolved. Tai chi said a practitioner should always be ready to shift her base if the floor gave way, to imagine she was stepping on thin ice about to break or that stones moved under her as she crossed a river.

Claire looked at the new glass on the other side of the cab and at the passenger's seat, where the stolen books had been, and felt she was stepping on unsteady stones. In the time since Burke's death, the ache had dulled, but it was still there. She sent her thoughts about Burke and the will into the air like trial balloons with strings attached. What if she were wrong about his death and Samantha were right? Could Mariah have gotten Burke outside under the cottonwood tree if he didn't want to go? If he'd objected, he could have raised his voice and woken Claire, who was just down the hallway. Would he have gone outside willingly in the middle of the night if he hadn't wanted to die? And how could Mariah have gotten away with pretending to be someone she wasn't? Wouldn't Burke have known whether or not she was his daughter? He had introduced her as his daughter and seemed perfectly rational when he did so. Another puzzle was why Burke had chosen Claire for the difficult job of being his personal representative. She released a balloon marked resentment into the air, but held onto one marked responsibility. He had trusted her, and she couldn't let him down. When the estate was settled, maybe she would get in her truck and go somewhere. She might even leave her truck behind and return to Europe. It would be interesting to travel around Europe again with the Mediterranean at her side. She had never been back in all these years.

When she reached Reserve, she stopped at the bank and made arrangements to access Burke's account, and then she went to the sheriff's office. She was relieved to find Sheriff Henner sitting at his desk and not out cruising the back roads of Catron County.

Henner stood up when he saw her and extended his bear paw hand. "Ms. Reynier. What are you doing in Reserve?"

"I'm settling up matters with the Lovell estate."

The sheriff smiled, turning his face into a maze of wrinkles, cracked and dry as the desert floor. "You have your work cut out for you with that family. I got the copy of the will, by the way. Thanks for sending it."

"You're welcome. How's the investigation coming?"

"The DA hasn't decided whether or not he's going to prosecute. He's waiting to get the drug screen back. The daughter from Santa Fe was in here angry as a hornet. I don't know as I blame her now that I've seen the will. Mariah's an outsider in Catron County. Some people will hold that against her. Still, here we believe a man's got a right to choose how and when he wants to die. But like I said, it's up to the DA. Give my regards to Corinne while you're in the Blue."

"I'll do that," Claire said.

As she drove down the dirt road into the Blue, Claire thought of the Spanish word *caracol,* meaning snail, spiral staircase, winding road. Snow was melting in the higher elevations. The river was up and rushing under the bridge to the ranch. There would be no footing at all on the stones today. As she crossed the bridge, Claire saw a woman on horseback galloping across the field. The woman seemed perfectly attuned to the rhythms of the horse. Watching her, Claire could understand how the Native Americans, who had never seen a horse before the Spaniards arrived, had the impression that horse and rider were one. Her childhood had been full of music lessons, dancing lessons, and tennis lessons, but she hadn't gone through a horse phase, unlike most of her girlfriends, or ever considered the possibility that she and a horse could move as one. To her, a horse was a stubborn animal determined to dump her and race back to the stable to eat. After Dancer succeeded in throwing her into the mud, Claire never rode again.

She parked her truck near the house. The rider, Mariah, approached, pulling up on the reins and bringing the horse to a halt. The horse stood while Claire talked to Mariah, but it wasn't still. Its black coat was slick with sweat. It snorted and danced in place. This was the kind of horse that would have taken Claire's measure and thrown her immediately. Mariah's face was flushed. Her black hair tumbled loose around her head. "Good to see you," she said.

"How are you?" Claire replied.

"All right. Let me put Burr in the corral, and I'll meet you inside."

"Okay."

She was greeted at the front door by Corinne, who looked as if she hadn't eaten since the last time Claire was there, and a forlorn Roamer, whose long ears drooped closer to the ground. As soon as the door opened, Claire caught the odor of something cooking.

"It smells delicious," she said.

72

"I've been cooking for you."

"You didn't need to do that."

"I wanted to."

The women hugged. Claire bent over and scratched Roamer's head. "Are you all right, Corinne?"

"Getting by."

"Sheriff Henner says hello."

"You saw him in Reserve?"

"Yes."

"Where's Eric?"

"Taking a nap."

They went inside and sat down in the kitchen. Roamer flopped at Claire's feet. Corinne gave her a cup of hot cider with a stick of cinnamon. Claire breathed in the smell of the spice. "Did you get my letter about the will?" she asked.

Corinne nodded. "Yes."

"Samantha came to see me."

"I know." Corinne got up from the table and went to the stove, turning her back to Claire.

When Claire told her about the theft of the books, Corinne didn't respond. Claire asked if there was anything she'd like from Burke's collection, and Corinne replied, "Not really."

"What time is dinner?" Claire asked.

"Around six. I'm cooking a ham."

"Why don't I get started on the papers, then?"

"You know where the office is."

Claire left Corinne in the kitchen and walked through the living room, where the hunting trophies were staring blankly at the ashes in the fireplace. There was no fire burning in the woodstove in the library, and the room seemed cold and empty. Her footsteps echoed as she walked across the bare floor. The books on the shelves had provided soundproofing and insulation. She had expected to find the shelves still empty, but some of them had been taken over by squatters: fat ceramic figurines and frilly dolls, the kind of trite knickknacks that made Claire squirm. There was printed material on the shelves, too: paperbacks, hardcovers, and magazines, which she stopped to examine. The magazines were *Good Housekeeping, Martha Stewart's Living,* and *Redbook.* The hardcovers were cookbooks. The paperbacks were romances with Fabio (or Fabio clones) and big-breasted women in ripped bodices on the covers, books with tattered covers that would bring a quarter at a paperback exchange, books with plots that were so identical, the only reason to read them was to induce sleep. Someone had made their mark on Burke's den, and Claire supposed it was Corinne.

She hurried out of the library and into the office, where she found that the computer had been dusted and the top of the desk cleared. Had Burke ever been that organized? she wondered. Or had someone been in here cleaning and rearranging his things? She'd been comfortable packing Burke's books in the library, but she felt like an intruder in the office. Still, it was something that had to be done, and the sooner she got started, the sooner she would finish. She straightened her back, opened the drawers, and began examining the files.

When Corinne called her to dinner, Claire had found Burke's copy of the will, a folder of bills that needed to be paid, bank books, checks, and a stock portfolio. The liquid assets were as he had said—eight hundred thousand dollars, two hundred thousand for each devisee. There were no mortgage statements for the ranch, indicating he'd owned it free and clear. Claire found the insurance policy and an appraisal establishing the ranch's value at two million dollars, even more than she had expected. The only important paper she couldn't locate was the deed to the ranch.

"Do you know where your father kept the deed?" she asked Corinne.

"No."

"Did he have a safe here or a safe deposit box at the bank?"

"Not that I know of."

They sat down for dinner under the antler chandelier along with Jed, Mariah, and Eric. The baked ham had been cured with something smoky and sweet, and was delicious. Eric chattered away, but the adults said little. Claire wondered how these people could eat together night after night without talking. There are three ways of being, she thought. The best is to live with someone you love. The second best is to live alone but have good friends. The third (and worst) is to live with someone you can't stand or have nothing in common with.

When dinner was over, Claire asked Mariah to meet her in the living room after she put Eric to bed. While she waited, she started a fire in the stone fireplace, then sat in front of it, absorbing the warmth and trying to ignore the glassy eyes of the antelope and buffalo at her back.

"I expected to find you in the library," Mariah said when she showed up. "I call this the dead animal room. I'm going to take them out of here once this house is mine."

"They do have a presence," Claire replied. "But the library has a different feeling now that Burke's books are gone. I feel even less comfortable there."

"Corinne has left her mark."

"Who would have thought it would be so . . ." Claire searched for the right word. Insipid? Banal? "Domestic," she said.

"Corinne is a domestic person."

"How is it working out with the two of you living here without Burke?"

"Fine," Mariah said. "She has her interests, I have mine. She stays in the library and the kitchen. I spend a lot of time outside. She's good with Eric."

Mariah sat down in a leather chair on the other side of the fire. The rest of the room receded into the shadows. It was as good a time as any to talk about difficult things. "Did you get my letter about the will?"

Mariah's eyes reflected back the flame. "Yes."

"Samantha came to see me. The family is very unhappy about the terms."

"I know."

"They're talking about contesting it."

"On what grounds?"

"That Burke was under the influence of drugs and alcohol, and not competent when he signed it."

"That's not true."

Claire looked into the fire and found encouragement in the leaps of the flames. "Samantha also believes you are not who you say you are."

"Meaning?"

"That you are not Burke's daughter."

"That's a lie!" Mariah's eyes were bright, her cheeks flushed. "And I can prove it." She jumped out of her chair and ran from the room.

The fire had gotten too hot, and Claire pushed her chair back. An advantage to a woodstove was that it was easier to control the flow of air and dampen the flame. The fireplace damper was over the flames and unreachable at this point. This fire would just have to burn hot until it burned itself out. In a few minutes Mariah came back with a folded-up document that she handed to Claire.

She unfolded the paper, a photocopy of a birth certificate stating Mariah's date of birth as March 3, 1971. The place of birth was Tucson. The mother's name was Kathleen Geraty, and the father was listed as Burke P. Lovell.

"Did Burke see this?" Claire asked.

"Yes. I showed it to him as soon as I got here. He was surprised, but very happy I had come."

"What happened between your mother and Burke?"

"I don't know. My mother would never talk about it and neither would Burke. She took me to California right after I was born. I didn't know who my father was until she told me just before she died. She wanted me to come back here and live on the ranch. She loved it here, and she knew I would, too. She said I had this place in my blood."

"Samantha told me you wouldn't take a DNA test."

"Why should I have to take a test?" Mariah's temper flared. Claire saw more of the Irish mother in her at that point than Burke Lovell. "Samantha is inheriting property, too, and no one is asking *her* to take a DNA test. How do we know that *she* is Burke's daughter?"

"Can I keep this?" Claire indicated the birth certificate.

Mariah nodded. "I have a copy."

"The one document I couldn't find in Burke's papers was the deed to the ranch. Do you have any idea where he kept it? I think if he had a safe deposit box, I would have found a key somewhere."

"I don't know," Mariah said.

"I've made an offer to the rest of the family that I'd like to make to you. Is there anything you want from Burke's book collection?"

"A personal history of one of the pioneer women."

"How about Susan McGoffin?"

"That would be great."

"I put some of my favorite books in a separate box, and it was stolen from my truck after I got back to the library." Claire watched Mariah to see what kind of a reaction this statement would get. Mariah's porcelain skin, which responded to every change in atmosphere, showed no sign of emotion.

"I'm sorry to hear that," she said. "Is there any way to get them back?"

"I'm trying."

"How?" Her eyes danced with curiosity.

"By talking to people I know in the trade." It was as much as Claire was willing to reveal.

Mariah yawned. "Anything else? Riding Burr all afternoon makes me want to go to bed early."

"That's all," Claire said.

Mariah went to bed, but Claire sat in her chair, staring at the flames until the fire burned out.

She went to bed in the downstairs guest room and woke up in the middle of the night, for she had to go to the bathroom. The room was freezing cold, so she stayed under the warm covers, hoping the urge would go away. It didn't, and when she could wait no longer, she got out of bed and padded down the hallway in her stocking feet. The bathroom door was open a crack, and the light was on reaching out across the hallway floor. This was the bathroom that Burke had used. Claire felt like she was in a dream and that if she looked through the crack, she would see Burke inside. She remembered how after her father had died, he appeared over and over in her dreams, trying to tell her something she could never understand.

You're being stupid, she said to herself. You were in here earlier. You must have left the light on before you went to bed.

Before she pushed the door open any farther, she looked through the crack and saw Corinne wearing a long flannel nightgown, standing beside the sink, hunched over it like an old woman. The sleeves of the nightgown were pushed up above her elbows. Corinne held a razor blade in her hand, and with a quick sharp motion made nicks in her forearm. Blood oozed from the wounds. Corinne was absorbed in the cutting and showed no signs of feeling any pain or of hearing Claire. The floor was littered with wads of bloody toilet paper.

Claire stopped breathing as she witnessed this act as private as masturbation, as terrifying as suicide. She feared that if she startled Corinne, the razor would slip, the cut would go deeper, and the blood would spurt from her arm. She also feared the effect of discovery on Corinne's mental state. If she walked away, Corinne might slit her wrists, but Claire didn't believe that was what cutters did. She knew it as an act of self-mutilation from which the perpetrator drew a twisted sense of control and an adrenaline rush that blocked the pain.

She stepped quietly across the hall into Burke's room, where she waited behind the door listening for Corinne to fall down or cry out. For a while there was silence and then the sound of water running and the toilet flushing. The light went out, and Claire heard Corinne walk down the hallway. She waited several minutes to give her time to go back to bed, then Claire entered the bathroom, shutting the door before turning on the light. The bathroom was sparkling clean, and there was no sign that anyone had been in here spilling her own blood. Corinne had cleaned up after herself and flushed the evidence down the toilet.

Claire went to the bathroom, then returned to bed but not to sleep. The scene she had witnessed held her with the force of a nightmare. She tried putting it in some kind of rational perspective. Corinne felt unloved and rejected by her father, scorned by others. The father had been too powerful and too feared for Corinne to express her resentment toward him, so she got in the habit of taking it out on herself. Claire spent hours chasing those thoughts around the bed.

She fell asleep finally, and at daybreak woke up to the smell of coffee. She dressed and went into the kitchen, where Corinne was standing at the stove with the sleeves of her nightgown pulled down to her wrists. "Good morning," she said, seeming wan but rested.

Claire supposed the cutting had been cathartic, and Corinne had slept deeply afterward, but witnessing it had left her feeling ragged. "Good morning," she answered. She poured herself a cup of coffee and sat down at the kitchen table.

"You know, Corinne, I felt depressed after my father died, and I went to a therapist in Tucson. I could give her your name if you ever feel you want to talk to somebody." Claire felt that to go any further might shatter the glass house of Corinne's privacy. Or was it the glass house of her own reserve?

"I don't want to talk to anybody," Corinne said, turning her back and stirring the hash browns on the stove.

"She was a big help to me," Claire said.

Corinne shook her head and kept on stirring.

Through the window Claire saw Jed walking by. "Does Jed drink coffee?" she asked.

"Yes."

"How does he like it?"

"Black."

"I'll take him a cup."

Claire poured a coffee for Jed, took a couple of quick swallows from her own mug, and went outside hoping the cold air would clear the cobwebs from her head.

"Thank you, ma'am," Jed said when she handed him the coffee.

"Can we talk?"

"Sure."

They walked to the end of the porch where a couple of idle rocking chairs waited, and sat down.

"Beautiful morning, isn't it?" Jed asked.

Mist rose from the gurgling river. A raven squawked and flew overhead. The air was fresh and cold. "It is," Claire agreed.

"Pleasure to be here on a day like this."

"You love this place, don't you?"

"Sure do."

"I wonder if you could help me with something."

"I'll try." Jed sipped at his coffee and stared at the river. He hadn't looked directly at Claire yet, which she attributed to shyness.

"Samantha tells me that the rest of the family is unhappy that Burke left Mariah the ranch."

"They're busy in Santa Fe and Phoenix. They never spend any time here." Jed kept his eyes on the middle distance. "But Mariah loves this place. She's a strong woman—the only one who's not afraid to ride Burr."

"And Corinne?"

"I don't know. It's hard to tell what moves Corinne. I think she'd sooner live here than any place else. The rest of the world scares her. But that's not the same as loving the place."

"You witnessed Burke's signature. Do you think he was incompetent or under the influence when he signed the will?"

"No, ma'am. I think he knew what he was doing. He wanted Mariah to have the ranch." Jed finished his coffee, put the mug down on the wooden boards of the porch, and squirmed in his rocking chair like a child getting ready to ask, "Can I go now?"

"You want to get back to work?"

He nodded.

"Thanks for your help."

"Glad to do it," he said, springing out of the chair. The rocker continued to rock while he hopped down the stairs, loped across the yard, and disappeared into the barn. Claire steadied his chair with her hand and got up carefully, leaving her rocker standing still.

She went back to Burke's office and gathered up the papers she thought she'd need. She'd been through the papers, she'd talked to Corinne, Mariah, and Jed. There was no reason to stay except to help Corinne, and Claire didn't know how she could. When she went to the kitchen, Corinne was sitting at the table with Mariah, helping Eric eat his cereal.

"Mariah," she said, "could you help me with something in the office?"

"Okay," Mariah got up and followed her.

"I'm worried about Corinne," Claire said when they were safely away from the kitchen. "Does she seem all right to you?"

"She's been down about Burke's death—we all have—but I think she's coping."

"Does she ever leave the ranch?"

"She has a friend in Reserve. She goes up there sometimes and spends the night."

"Keep an eye on her for me, will you? Let me know if she seems to be getting more depressed."

"All right."

Claire's truck pulled her out of the Blue and back to the highway. At one point she looked down into the valley and saw Burr pacing his corral. The road to Albuquerque seemed full of obstacles. Ravens picked at the bones of a coyote in the middle of Route 180. North of Quemado, cattle that were being herded from one end of a ranch to another forced the truck to a standstill while they swarmed around her like water. Construction brought traffic to a halt on the Rio Grande Bridge. In her weariness she saw the orange barrels that marked the lanes with an hallucinatory intensity.

CHAPTER SEVEN

When she got home, Claire checked the mail and the call screening box, let the cat out, and logged onto America Online. There were twenty messages. Sherry@hotmail.com promised, "You won't regret it cum and see." Steve@aol offered, "Health, Financial Freedom, and Free Cars." Earl@Rte66.com said, "Turn your washing machine into a cash cow." There was nothing here that made Claire want to read any further. A smiling face had not responded to her frown. No one was offering to sell her *The Brave Cowboy.* She deleted all her messages without opening any of them, and spent the rest of the weekend practicing tai chi, reading, and watching figure skating on TV.

On Monday morning before work, she called Tamara Hess, the therapist she knew in Tucson, to ask her advice about Corinne. "Cutting doesn't usually lead to attempted suicide or violence against others," Tamara said. "There are people who have been doing it for thirty years. They have to keep going deeper and deeper, and eventually they can sever an artery or a vein. She needs help. Can you get her to come in to see me or someone close to where she lives?"

"I don't know if there is anyone closer," Claire said. "She lives in the Blue."

"Maybe not," Tamara agreed.

"Should I have intervened? It seemed to be such a private act."

"Cutters are deep in denial. Sometimes they let their wounds fester until they smell. She might resent interference from an outsider, but what about the family?"

"I'll see what I can do," Claire replied, but she wasn't optimistic; everyone else in the Lovell family seemed mired in their own problems.

When she got to her desk at the library, she found a voice mail from Walter Massey. She was debating whether to call him back, when Ruth poked her head through the door to ask how the investigation was going.

"Nothing new," Claire said.

"If the books don't turn up soon"—Ruth laughed—"we'll have to send out the posse."

"Is Harrison getting anxious?" In her job Ruth had to deal with Harrison on a daily basis, whereas Claire was able to keep her distance.

"He'd be happier if the books were back in the library."

"So would I."

Ruth tipped her head to the side, a sign she was about to ask a question. "Where did you get the window of your truck fixed?"

"At the Chevy dealer."

"Did they do a good job?"

"Yes, and their courtesy van brought me back and forth to work. Why?"

"Gail wrecked her car last year. Since then she's been having problems with it that no one has been able to fix. I had to give her a ride to work this morning."

"She doesn't have a Chevy, does she?" Claire remembered Gail's car as being a small brown hatchback scarred by scratches, pockmarked by dings.

"No, a Honda."

"She ought to take it to the Honda dealer."

"I think she owes them money."

The comment surprised Claire, since she was convinced Gail

made more money than she did, and she never had any problems taking care of her truck. "Didn't she have insurance?"

"It was an older car; she'd let the collision insurance lapse." Ruth looked at her watch. "I have a meeting," she said. "Gotta run."

"Talk to you later," replied Claire.

She watched *Huckleberry Finn* and *Portrait of a Lady* sprout wings and fly across her computer screen while she called Walter Massey, who wanted to make a date for lunch.

"I have my own lawyer, and she'll probably want to come along," Claire replied.

"Who is it?"

"Sally Froelich."

"Oh, sure. I know Sally. She and I go way back."

"So she said."

"You name the time and the place."

"How about Thursday at noon at the Artichoke Café?" It was a restaurant Claire liked that was located right across the street from a public library devoted to genealogy, one of her favorite places in Albuquerque.

"See you there," Massey said.

On Thursday morning, Sally called to say something had come up that would require her presence in court all day and she'd have to cancel the lunch date.

"Should I go without you?" Claire asked.

"It's up to you. I think you can handle Massey, and it might be interesting to hear what he wants. He's liable to be more forthcoming if I'm not there. When two lawyers get together, sometimes all you get is legalese."

"All right," said Claire, thinking it would be good to get the meeting over with.

"Don't reveal any secrets or make any promises."

"I won't," Claire said.

The Artichoke Café turned out to be a good choice; Massey was obviously uncomfortable there. Claire supposed he would have been more at home at the Petroleum Club or the Black Angus Steak House. After a few minutes with Massey, Claire began to relish seeing him uncomfortable. The Artichoke Café was a small restaurant with tables squeezed close together, and Walter Massey was a big man. He stood over six feet tall and weighed at least two hundred pounds. His suit might have been expensive, but to Claire it looked sleazy, and she wasn't impressed by the size of the diamond in his ring. She sat on a banquette in the corner, and he sat across from her in a chair that was too small for him. While they ate, he shifted his weight from one corner of the chair to another, as if the legs were uneven and he couldn't keep his balance.

"What is it you do at Zimmerman Library?" he asked.

"I'm in charge of collection development."

"Oh?"

"I buy books for the Center for Southwest Research."

"I graduated from UNM."

"Did you?"

The waitress delivered a basket of bread and took their order. "Burke Lovell must have thought well of you to make you his personal representative." Massey tore the end off the loaf of bread and bit into it.

"We were friends for a long time," Claire replied.

"Settling an estate is a big job."

"Sally helps."

"I'm sorry she couldn't join us."

When the food arrived, Massey looked at his plate and commented, "I like my meat with a little more char on it than that," but he ate it anyway. He had ordered lamb, the only red meat on the menu. As he cut into it, bloody juice spread across his plate, staining his mashed potatoes pink. He finished first and leaned back in his chair thinking, Claire suspected as she ate her pasta, of a big, fat cigar, but this was a smoke-free restaurant. As soon as she put her fork down, he began to question her. "Were you present when Lovell signed the will?"

"Yes."

"I have information that he was incapacitated at the time."

"That's not true."

"No?" Massey leaned across his plate, hunching up his broad shoulders like a vulture picking over a carcass.

"No."

"I have a sworn affidavit from the nurse Kassandra Wells saying that Lovell was stumbling and slurring his words."

"How did you get her to say that?"

"She volunteered."

The waitress came around offering a desert cart and coffee. Massey took a cherry tart, but Claire had lost her appetite.

"My clients also don't believe that Mariah is Burke's daughter."

"He believed she was. She believes she is."

"Can she prove it?"

"She has a birth certificate."

Massey's tart left a cherry stain at the edge of his mouth. Claire was tempted to lift her napkin and wipe it off. "A birth certificate can be faked. A DNA test would prove or disprove paternity without a doubt."

"No one else has volunteered to take a DNA test."

"The other children were acknowledged from birth. They didn't show up suddenly when they were twenty-five years old."

"The will says Burke is leaving the ranch to Mariah Geraty," Claire countered, "not his daughter Mariah Geraty, so in terms of the will I don't know that paternity is relevant."

"It is if Mariah deceived Lovell and obtained her inheritance under false pretenses."

"I don't believe that."

Massey finished his cake and wiped his mouth, transferring the cherry stain to his napkin. "I don't need to remind you that there are considerable assets at stake here. A couple of million for the ranch, eight hundred thousand dollars in stocks. If we go to court, your testimony could keep that ranch from my clients."

"My testimony and Jed's."

"He's a ranch hand. You're a librarian."

Suggesting what? Claire wondered. That her profession gave her testimony more weight than Jed's?

"Are you positive Burke was of sound mind?" Massey leaned back in his chair. "Perhaps if you were willing to reconsider, you would see it differently." He left a question mark hanging over the table, a question mark that could easily be converted to a dollar sign.

He wasn't quite crude enough to say that librarians don't make much money, but Claire suspected him of thinking it. Her temper flared. "There's nothing to reconsider," she snapped. "I knew Burke well, and I know what I saw. He was not under the influence or incompetent when he signed that will. If need be, I'm willing to sign an affidavit to that effect."

Massey threw up his hands. "Hey, no need to get angry. Just wanted to be sure is all."

"I'm sure," Claire said.

The bill arrived in a green folder. Massey took his credit card from his wallet, inserted it into the folder, and the meal was over.

The genealogical library was in a Spanish Colonial–style building across the street. Claire could have happily spent the afternoon there retracing the steps of her Reynier ancestors, who arrived in New Amsterdam on a ship called *The Gilded Otter* in 1652. It would have been a pleasant diversion after the lunch with Walter Massey, but she had to get back to work.

When she reached her office, she called and left a message for Sally Froelich. Then she called Kassandra Wells in Reserve, obtaining her number from information. Kass had not yet taken another nursing job, and Claire found her at home. Once she heard who was calling, her vocal chords seemed to atrophy.

"I just had lunch with the Lovell family lawyer, who tells me you signed an affidavit stating Burke Lovell was under the influence when he signed the will," Claire said.

There was a pause while Kassandra cleared her throat. "That's how I saw it."

"You know that's not true, Kass. He was perfectly rational all afternoon and through dinner."

"He'd been drinking Jack Daniel's and taking Valium," Kass insisted.

"He had a shot of Jack Daniel's at dinner, and if he had taken any Valium at that point, he gave no sign of it."

"That's not what I saw." Kass began digging in her heels.

Claire wondered if she was getting paid to say this, but she didn't see any point of antagonizing Kass by accusing her of selling out. She and Jed agreed that Burke was of sound mind. That was two out of three, which ought to be enough, even if she was a librarian and he was a ranch hand. "If you change your mind, call me." Claire gave her number.

"I won't be changing my mind." Kass hung up.

Sally got out of court early and called an hour later. When Claire told her about the lunch with Walter Massey and the conversation with Kass Wells, her response was "Pass the Rolaids, please."

"Do you think they paid Kass to lie?" Claire asked.

"It's either a carrot or a stick. I gather Massey was getting ready to offer you money, too. There's plenty of it to go around now, but there won't be when he gets through."

"I find his suggestion offensive."

"It's his business to be offensive. That's why his clients pay him the big bucks."

"He implied that the will could be negated if Mariah deceived Burke about being his daughter."

"It's a possibility. Does she have any proof?"

"She gave me a copy of her birth certificate with Burke listed as her father."

"Could you send me a copy?"

"Sure."

"Have you heard from the genealogical search company yet?"

"No."

"Let's wait till we hear from them before we do anything. If they establish without a doubt that Burke is Mariah's father, that could clip Massey's wings."

Claire spent the rest of the afternoon sorting through the Porter photos, deciding which ones to exhibit. It was a tough choice as they were all beautiful, ranging from shimmering red canyons reflected in the Colorado River to violets on the floor of an Appalachian forest. Late in the day she got a call from John Harlan, an antiquarian bookseller she knew in Albuquerque. You can take the man out of Texas, but you can't take Texas out of the man, she thought as she listened to John's drawl.

He was one of Claire's favorite book people. In midlife he sold the oil business he'd inherited in Midland, Texas, moved to Santa Fe, opened a bookstore specializing in Western Americana, blew all his oil money on books, and was happier losing money in New Mexico than he'd ever been making it in Texas. No one who loved books ever went to Santa Fe without making a pilgrimage to John's store. He developed an encyclopedic knowledge of Western Americana, and was always happy to talk about it. Then his beloved wife Jane died, and he didn't want to run the business without her. He sold the inventory and retired for a second time, but book people rarely stay retired. It's a lifelong addiction that can lead to poverty and bankruptcy, yet the addict keeps coming back for more.

"Well, what the hell, I'm not beatin' anybody up or hurtin' the environment," John liked to say. "All I'm doin' is blowin' the family fortune, and I got nobody to leave that to anyway." He spent his year in retirement rereading Zane Grey, and then he took a job at Page One, Too, a bookstore in Albuquerque that was expanding into the rare-book business.

"Hey, Claire, John here," he said. "How's it going in academentia?"

"Not too bad," Claire replied.

"I don't use that damn Internet myself, but Marie, who works for me, got an offer this afternoon you ought to know about. Damn, I hate that e-mail. When I communicate with someone, I like to see 'em face-to-face, not be lookin' at little gray letters. I don't even like the telephone. This person only identified himself or herself by a bunch of numbers. Five of 'em to be exact. I don't even know if it's a man or a woman. Anyway the message said the person had a *Brave Cowboy* to sell and a *Blessing Way* and a *Death Comes for the Archbishop.* Now, what the hell does that sound like to you?"

"My books."

"That's what I'm thinkin'. What do you want me to do?"

"Find out what else they have, offer to buy the books, lure the seller into the store."

"I'd say we're lookin' at six thousand dollars worth of books right here. But if we're talking all the books, it's gonna be quite a bit more. If they do have all the books, can you come up with the money? Much as I admire what you're doin', Claire, I'm not in a position to be a benefactor of the library."

"I might be able to get it from the library's or Burke's insurance, but I have a better idea. I've been working with a university police-woman. Maybe she would set up a sting."

"That would get you the thief and the books. Want me to see if I can get any more information out of this SOB?"

"Let me."

"How?"

"Ask Marie to forward me the e-mail message." Claire gave him her address at the library. "I'll compose a query asking what else they have and drop it by on my way home from work. Marie can e-mail it to the seller in the morning. Will you be there after five?"

"Have you ever known me to go home before five?"

"Never."

"I'm not gonna disappoint you now."

They said their good-byes and got off the phone.

Claire was elated that the books might have surfaced, and she wanted to run down the hallway and tell everyone. But there was still the possibility that the thefts had been an inside job. It would be better if no one but John Harlan and Rachel Dunbar knew a contact had been made. Claire called Rachel and passed on the news.

"Glad to hear it," Rachel said. "My investigation has been going nowhere."

"If the seller has our books and John can get him or her into the store, would you be willing to set up a sting?"

"I'd love to try."

"That's assuming, of course, a thief would be dumb enough to come into the store."

"Well, it doesn't take a genius to break a window and steal a box of books. It's hard to underestimate the intelligence of the average crook. When I worked for the APD, we were thrilled if we ever found a criminal who thought about the act for more than five minutes. In your average crime, some scumbag gets drunk, gets mad, fires a gun, and somebody else catches the bullet."

"I'll let you know what develops."

"You do that," Rachel said.

By the time Claire got off the phone with Rachel, her computer told her she had e-mail. Marie had forwarded the query which read, "I have copies of *The Brave Cowboy, A Thief of Time, Death Comes for the Archbishop,* and others for sale. Are you interested?"

"Very," Claire said to the screen.

She went to Netscape and ran a reverse search on Five Numbers screen name—26688@anon.net.fi—but she wasn't optimistic. She knew anon.net.fi to be a service in Finland that provided e-mailers with an anonymous address. There were days when a computer could be as stubborn as a husband, and she waited impatiently for an answer. Eventually e-mail finder told her what she expected— there were no listings to match her search criteria. With anon.net.fi, the query could have come from anybody anywhere.

"Damn," Claire said to herself.

She composed an answer, rewriting her response several times to get the wording just right. She settled on, "Very interested. We are expanding our Southwestern fiction section. If you have any more Hillermans or Abbeys or Cathers, we'd also be interested in them." She closed with John Harlan's name.

After work, she drove home by way of Montgomery, stopping at Page One, Too. The store was a warren of bookshelves. John's office was tucked away in a far corner of the building with a window looking out on the parking lot. Claire peeked in, saw he was on the phone, and grazed the Southwest section looking to see if there was anything she or the library didn't already own.

John called her into his office when he got off the phone. He had the lean, alert look of a greyhound retired from racing but still ready to jump at the sight of a rabbit. Although he was six feet tall, he didn't weigh much more than Claire. When she hugged him, she felt she was pulling something ephemeral back to earth. The bookshelves in his office overflowed. Every flat surface was covered with unshelved books, catalogs, and price guides. There were several styrofoam cups with the dregs of coffee at the bottom, left there by people who had visited John during the day. He saw more people in the course of one day than anyone else Claire knew. There was a computer on his desk, but he hadn't bothered to turn it on yet.

"Pleasure to see you, Claire."

"You, too."

"Did you bring the message for Five Numbers?"

"I did," Claire replied, showing it to him.

John scratched his head. "You didn't have any more Cathers in that box, did you?"

"And if this person is our thief, he or she won't have any more, either."

"Not necessarily. A book dealer might."

"Do you think a dealer would offer the books to you? You're awfully close to the theft."

"Books tend to gravitate to where they'll get the most money."

"Wouldn't a dealer have given a better description of the books? The query didn't say that the books were in fine condition, that they were first editions, that the Hillerman was illustrated, that the Abbey had an inscription, that the Cather was the limited edition."

"It might be a professional trying to throw us off the trail by acting like an amateur. There's only one way to find out for sure. Make a low-ball offer."

"You always make a low offer."

"And nobody who knows what they're doing ever accepts. All right with you if I have Marie send that message out in the morning? She doesn't keep the kind of hours I do."

"That's fine."

John contemplated the dust on his computer screen. "You doin' anything for dinner?"

"Going home and boiling some pasta."

"Would you like to stop at Emilios?"

"Sounds good."

"Let me close up here." Closing up meant picking up his jacket, saying good-bye to the people at the counter, and walking out the door.

Claire met him at Emilio's, where they got two bowls of spaghetti that were large enough to feed six people. John rolled his spaghetti on his fork and talked about people they knew and books between bites. He cleaned his plate, but Claire asked for a doggy bag, something she never did while dining out with Evan. Evan refused to eat leftovers.

As if he'd read her mind, John brought up the subject of her ex-husband. "You and Evan got a divorce?"

"Yes."

"Sorry to hear that."

"It was for the best." John and his wife Jane had a long and successful marriage. When Claire looked across the table, she could see the ghost of Jane at his side. She wondered if he could imagine what it was like to live with someone with whom you were basically incompatible.

He looked up at her with an unexpectedly hopeful and admiring expression. Claire recognized the look from that time long ago when she dated. She hadn't seen it for so long, she'd almost forgotten. She and John were both alone now, but she had known him too long with Jane to think of him as a single. Claire wouldn't expect John to make a pass, but he might make a polite inquiry.

She looked at her watch. "I'd better be getting home."

"I'll call you as soon as I get a reply from Five Numbers," he said.

"Thanks," she replied.

When Claire got home, Nemesis rubbed against her legs and meowed, making it plain he wanted to go out. However, it was the hour when the coyotes began loping down Bear Canyon and across Elena Gallegos Recreation Area, looking for a quick and easy meal. "Sorry," she said, picking the cat up and giving him a hug. Her son Michael liked to say that if he could be reincarnated, he'd come back as a single woman's cat; no other creature in the universe got so much attention. Claire put the cat down and prepared for bed.

There were floor-to-ceiling shelves in her bedroom full of books, some collectible, some just books that she liked. It made the walls as thick and impermeable as adobe and far more interesting than wallpaper or bare white minimalist walls hung with Southwestern art. Claire had the luxury of two fireplaces in her house. The one in her bedroom was fueled by gas and had ceramic logs that wouldn't splinter or turn to ash. The flame burned silently without a crackle or a hiss, and had the steady consistency of a pilot light never making the leaps and sparks of the fires she burned with wood. Gas was too predictable for Claire's taste; she preferred a wood fire, but she didn't have to stack the wood for her gas fireplace or take out the ashes. Best of all, the gas fire could be controlled by a remote. She could click it on from bed in the morning and off once she'd warmed up the bed.

Claire got into bed, and Nemesis curled up at her feet. She clicked the remote and watched the gas flames spring into action and lick the ceramic logs. It was time to read, but there was nothing on her bedside table at the moment. She considered the books on her shelves. They resembled the old friends with whom she had late-night phone conversations and shared her deepest thoughts. Her joy in reading came from discovering there was someone out there who had the same feelings and ideas she did but could express them better than she ever could. Books never turned cold and indifferent, didn't grow up and move away, get married to someone you didn't like, or trade you in for a newer model. Books were there when you needed them. In Claire's private library, the books went beyond the Southwest. She could pick *One Hundred Years of Solitude* off the shelf anytime, and Meme Buendía would be making love to Mauricio Babilonia, surrounded by yellow butterflies. She could continually be lost in the labyrinth of a Borges short story or suffer excruciating suspense over whom a Jane Austen heroine would marry. No matter how despicable the creepy Ripley became, Patricia Highsmith always made her want him to escape. She could turn to any page in her Raymond Chandler collection, confident that Philip Marlowe would find the perfect metaphor. She had recently added Arundhati Roy to her shelves, another master of metaphor. Claire slept better knowing her favorite characters and her favorite phrases were all in place on the shelves.

But as she drifted into the hallucinatory suburb that surrounded the city of sleep, she had the sense that her characters weren't staying in place on the shelves. That once she drifted off, they intended to get out of their books and wander. The query from the bookseller seemed too easy. Her last thought before she fell asleep was that she was missing something.

Five Numbers didn't respond to their e-mail the next day or the day after that. Claire knew that if the e-mail address had been incorrect, the message would have come back saying there was a permanent fatal error. Maybe the seller wasn't reading e-mail, or had gone out of town, or was playing a cat-and-mouse game with them; maybe that person was trying to sell the books to someone else. Claire hoped any dealer who got an offer would contact her, but she couldn't count on it. She checked her e-mail several times a day. In the morning she practiced the more calming tai chi exercises: cloud hands, playing the lute, white crane flaps wings, ending with the infinite ultimate stance.

Harrison stopped by her office to see how the investigation was coming.

"There's been a lead," Claire told him, "but nothing definite. Someone e-mailed Page One, Too, offering to sell *The Brave Cowboy, A Thief of Time,* and *Death Comes for the Archbishop.* We don't know yet if they're Burke's books. John Harlan e-mailed them back, trying to get more information, but we haven't gotten a response."

"There's no way to identify the e-mailer?"

"It came from one of those services that provides anonymity."

"Did you tell university police?"

"Yes."

"Have they been getting anywhere with their investigation?"

"No. They haven't ruled out the possibility that the thief works here, and I wouldn't want word to get out that I've been in contact with John. I'm afraid the thief would crawl under a rock if he or she knew, and we'd never get the books back."

Harrison had picked up a glass paperweight from her desk and was turning it over and over in his long hands. "Of course," he said, putting the paperweight down. "Keep me informed."

Later in the day Claire ran into Gail in the hallway to the ladies' room. The hallway was narrow, and one person needed to step aside to let the other pass. The issue of who stepped aside could be awkward. Some people pulled rank, some people tried very hard not to. Gail avoided the issue by looking at the floor and sidling close to the wall. Her face had a pinched expression, and she wore a baggy brown dress. Claire could have squeezed by, but Gail stopped and asked about the book investigation.

"Nothing new," Claire felt obligated to reply, hoping Harrison had kept his promise not to discuss the e-mail query with Gail or anyone else. "How's your car? Ruth said you've been having problems." Gail had been out sick, and their paths hadn't crossed since Claire's conversation with Ruth.

"The one thing you can count on when your life turns to shit is that your car won't run," Gail said.

What could be wrong with Gail's life? Claire wondered. Money problems? Men problems? Health problems? Rivals at work problems? "Is something wrong?" she asked.

A curtain opened in Gail's eyes, and for an instant Claire could see that something was very wrong, but the curtain quickly closed again. "No," Gail said. "Ever since the accident, it's been one thing after another with the car. Now it's an electrical problem. It starts up all by itself while sitting in the driveway. It stops dead in the middle of traffic. The lights go off and on with no rhyme or reason. I've found a new mechanic who thinks he can fix it."

"Good luck." Claire said, wondering why—with interest rates as low as they were—Gail didn't just buy a new car. She'd seen Nissans advertised for as little as one hundred dollars a month.

"Thanks," Gail said, scurrying down the hall like a mouse that's been spooked by a hawk in the sky.

CHAPTER EIGHT

The next time John called, Claire was sitting at her desk trying to decipher an obscure memo from Harrison, which began with the pompous phrase, "To be sure," and went on to say "my deliberations on the subject have led me to conclude that it would be in the best interests of everyone concerned to weigh carefully all of the options presented." Any memo that began with a sentence like that belonged in the round file, and that was where it was headed. How could someone use so many words to say so little? Claire wondered. Words were the tools of the librarian's trade, and one would have thought that command of the English language would be the first requirement for Harrison's job.

Fortunately, John Harlan always got right to the point. "Hey, Claire," he said. "I received another communiqué from Five Numbers asking me to make an offer on all of the books."

"All of them?"

"Well, let's see there's *Ben Hur*, *Red Sky at Morning*, *Ride the Pink Horse....*" While he read off the list of books, Claire compared it to her own and saw a gaping hole.

"It's all the novels," she said. "But not all the books."

"What's missing?"

"The Austin/Adams folio."

"Damn," John swore in his Texas drawl. "How in the hell did I miss that? I was so excited about gettin' the books back, I must have skipped right over it. I haven't seen one of those folios on the market for years. It must be worth, oh, hell, I'd say eighteen thousand dollars anyhow."

"Thirty or more," Claire replied.

"Well, now, that depends on whether you're buyin' or sellin'. In this case we're buyin', and when I buy, I rarely pay more than sixty percent of retail. I have to make a profit somehow."

"*The History of the Blue* is missing, too."

"Who's gonna give a hoot about that book? Every small town in the West has a self-proclaimed historian who self-publishes a history. Nobody reads 'em but the author's mother. I've had *The History of the Blue* on my shelf for years, and I haven't been able to sell it. I'm considerin' putting it in my discount bin. What do you think the novels are worth?"

Claire, who had already calculated the books value, subtracted the folio and came up with, "Twenty thousand."

"Kind of steep, isn't it?"

"The *Ben Hur* is inscribed to Pat Garrett. A Billy the Kid collector could be willing to pay a lot for that book."

"Even so, that's a retail price. If I offer that much, anyone who knows anything about books is gonna know I'm workin' with you."

"Then, offer sixty percent."

"Or fifty to allow some negotiating room."

"I don't want to dicker, John. I just want the books back."

"Askin' a book dealer not to dicker is like askin' a coyote not to yip, but for you, Claire, I'll try. Is it your money?"

"Yes," Claire admitted. She had no guaranty that she'd be reimbursed by the insurance company, but getting the books back was so important to her she'd decided to pay for them herself.

"How about offering ten thousand depending on condition? We've got to see them before we pay for them. How else are we going to get the seller to come in? Are you sure you can identify the books?"

"They have fingerprint features like the inscriptions to Burke and Pat Garrett."

"If we keep the offer low, we're more likely to find out who we're dealing with. A dealer's not gonna accept a low offer even on stolen merchandise; it's just not their nature."

"Do you think a dealer is going to come walking into your store with a boxful of stolen books?"

"No. I think the dealer will send a representative. Let's compromise at eleven."

"All right."

"When I e-mail Five Numbers back, do you want me to ask about the missing books?"

"Then, they'd know for sure you're working with me."

"I don't think anyone will sell the folio intact anyway. The prints are more valuable razored out and sold on the art market."

"I know." Claire sighed.

"I'll make the offer and see if I can lure the son of a bitch in. Are you going to tell those back stabbers at the library what we're up to?"

"Only the university policewoman I've been dealing with," Claire said.

She got off the phone with John and called Rachel, who was not in her office. Claire left a message on her beeper. Instead of calling back, Rachel showed up fifteen minutes later.

"I was at the food court, where there was a food fight going on," she said. "Students!" She sat down in the chair facing Claire's desk. "I hope you have something for me to work on besides fighting, drinking, and Rohypnol. Sometimes I feel like I'm Rohypnol cop."

"What's Rohypnol?"

"Roofies, Mexican Valium, the date-rape drug."

Claire picked up a pencil and turned it over in her fingers. "John Harlan at Page One, Too got an e-mail offer to sell all the stolen novels."

Rachel's sharp eyes focused on Claire. "But not all the books?"

"No. If he can lure the seller into the store, can you set up a sting?"

"Sure," Rachel said.

"Will you do it all by yourself?"

"I'll have to. We don't have the staff here, and it's not likely I can interest the APD in a book theft. I have the authority to make arrests off campus as long as they are in Albuquerque."

"I'd like to be there."

Rachel shook her head. "Not a good idea. Could be the thief knows you. If they see your car in the parking lot, they'll never come in."

"I won't go in my own car. I can hide in the bathroom next to John's office. You'll need me to identify the books before you can make an arrest."

"There's a good chance the seller is—or is connected to—someone who works here. Are you prepared for that?"

Was she? Claire leaned against the back of her chair and straightened her shoulders. "Yes," she said.

"You'll need a convincing reason for your absence from the library."

"No problem; I'll say I'm looking at a book collection."

"All right, then," Rachel said. She stood up. "I'll have to visit the thrift stores on Central."

"Why?"

"To find a disguise." She looked down at her uniform. "I can't conduct a sting operation dressed like this." Rachel's beeper went off. She looked at the message, rolled her eyes, and said, "Something happening near the bookstore."

Claire had another long and boring meeting to attend. Rachel didn't know what her call would lead to, but Claire knew what to expect at the meeting. Her coworkers would spend an uncomfortable hour trying to communicate with each other. Her presence was required, but she didn't have much to contribute. She sat still as a stone while their words flowed around her.

"Not necessarily," Harrison said several times.

"Of course." Ruth provided the punctuation.

"Sure." Ralph was agreeable.

So was Celia. "Good idea."

"If you say so," mumbled Gail.

Harrison's long fingers unfolded and refolded the wings of a paper clip. Although he went through the motions of leading the meeting, his mind appeared to be wandering through a remote canyon. Ralph brushed the hair out of his eyes as he watched Harrison. Ruth's eyes flitted around the table, landing on Claire with a curious expression. Celia played with the buttons on her denim jacket. Gail was pale and nervous. Claire wondered which one of these people was likely to show up at Page One, Too, if Rachel was right. The smart money would go to Gail.

John Harlan e-mailed back and forth to Five Numbers, and the transaction date was finally set for the following Thursday. The price agreed on was eleven thousand dollars. The seller insisted on coming in exactly at 12:30. "On his or her lunch hour," according to John.

As soon as she had a date, Claire told her coworkers—beginning with Harrison—that she would be out of the office that day looking at a book collection in Santa Fe. "Anything interesting in it?" Harrison asked.

"There's a *Songs of the Cowboys*," she replied. It was the first collection of cowboy poetry, a book the library didn't have and one that Harrison coveted. "But I don't know what condition it's in." Since Claire wasn't used to lying, she was surprised by how fluently the words rolled off her tongue and by the lack of guilt she felt. Intuitively she sensed that the key to a successful lie was to divert the recipient's attention with details. Once Harrison heard *Songs of the Cowboys* was available, covetousness would keep him from hearing anything else.

By the time Thursday arrived, Claire had told all her coworkers she would be in Santa Fe and received no unusual reaction. She checked her e-mail often, but there were no messages regarding the books. Sleep became an elusive shadow that she spent long nights chasing around her bed. On Thursday morning, after hours of tossing and turning, she looked at the clock, saw it was five-thirty, and got up in the dark. She fed the cat, went into the den, and practiced tai chi. Was this a day for calming exercises, or for militancy? she asked herself. She felled the tree, punched the leopard, repulsed the monkey, and ended by embracing the tiger and skipping the infinite ultimate stance.

As soon as the banks were open, she drove to her Norwest branch and got a cashier's check for eleven thousand dollars. The seller had insisted on cash or cashier's check. The check was as good as cash, and carrying that much money around in her purse made Claire uncomfortable. She had arranged for a cab to pick her up at ten-thirty, and she clutched her purse on her lap while she directed the driver to the back door of Page One, Too. John was waiting, and as soon as they were in his office, she handed the check over to him. He glanced quickly at the amount, then stuffed it in his pocket.

"Right on time," he said, looking at the clock on his wall that ticked as loudly as the clocks did in grammar school.

Claire was always on time—sometimes even early—which put her at a disadvantage in a state with an elastic sense of time where events regularly started late. Charles Lummis had called it the Land of Poco Tiempo almost a hundred years ago, and in that respect New Mexico hadn't changed. John suggested that Claire arrive at noon, but she had wanted time to prepare herself. "Is Rachel here yet?" she asked.

"She is, but you may not be able to find her."

"Why not?" she asked.

"She's camouflaged pretty good."

"Have I got time to look?"

"Hell, Claire, Five Numbers isn't going to show up this early, hang around the store, and give us all the time in the world to get to know him or her."

"All right," Claire said. She left John's office and wandered through the bookshelves looking for Rachel, seeing the usual collection of badly dressed book buyers. People didn't dress up for parties in Albuquerque, and they sure weren't going to do it to look at secondhand books.

Claire watched a woman in the Southwest section pull a book off the shelf. She wore scuffed boots, a long denim skirt with a frayed hem, and a fringed suede vest. Her hair was pulled up in a knot and streaked with gray. She had on no makeup, unless it was a foundation that made her skin tone drab and sallow. She wore granny glasses. Before she looked at the book, she pushed the glasses on top of her head as if she had a second set of eyes there. It was Rachel thirty years down the road. Rachel as a flower child turning into a middle-aged woman, the type of person least likely to be suspected of a crime. Her body language was frail and tired. Her shoulders were stooped. She squinted as she studied the book. Claire was impressed by Rachel's acting skills, but discouraged by her concept of a book person. There was a mirror mounted high on the wall reflecting the aisle of books. Whoever manned the cash register could look into it and keep an eye on the customers. Rachel appeared in the mirror and so did Claire, but Claire had the image of a hunter, erect and alert. She was more excited by the prospect of catching the thief than she ever would have expected.

When Claire walked by, Rachel ignored her keeping her eyes focused on the book she held in her hands. A backpack lay at her feet. A backpack so close to the bookshelves could make any librarian or bookseller nervous. Claire wondered if she had a weapon in it.

When she got back to John's office, the clock on the wall said eleven-thirty, which gave her an hour to kill. John asked her what she intended to do while she waited.

"Read," she said. She picked a copy of a price guide off the mess on his desk and took it into the bathroom, which badly needed cleaning. The sink had a layer of grime. There was scum under the toilet. The light switch was outside in John's office.

"I don't think anybody's going to know you're in there, but just in case, I'll turn the light off at 12:15. All right?" John asked.

"All right."

Claire put the toilet seat down and sat on it trying to pay attention to the prices in the price guide, but her mind kept wandering to the missing books. She heard John's clock on the other side of the door ticking off the minutes with agonizing slowness. Tick. Stop. Tick. Stop. She tried to synchronize her breathing to its rhythm while she waited. Madelyn had once commented that you knew when it was the dark of the moon because phones stopped ringing and people stopped talking. Claire wondered if it were that time. John's phone, which usually rang all day, became still. All she could hear was the squeak of his chair and the ticking clock. Eventually John walked across the floor and flipped the light switch, signifying it was 12:15 and leaving Claire in a darkness so total she couldn't even see her fingers. Her mind peopled the darkness with the faces of her associates, and she wondered if one of them (or one of their representatives) would show up with her books. With nothing to look at, her other senses became more acute. The bathroom smelled. The clock ticked even louder. She didn't count the ticks, and she couldn't tell if fifteen minutes had passed or five. She waited, waited, and waited some more. There was nothing she hated more than waiting, and being trapped in a dark closet made it even more frustrating. John's chair creaked. He got up, and she heard his footsteps pacing the room. He, at least, had the option of pacing, but she didn't dare announce her presence by moving. Her feelings of excitement and apprehension peaked, then turned to despondency. She went from wondering who would turn up to fearing that no one would. Eventually she heard Rachel enter John's office and declare, "They're not coming." John yanked the door open, and the bathroom was invaded by the light.

"Damn," John said. "No one showed up."

Rachel stood behind John with the glasses perched on top of her head. "Something must have spooked 'em."

"Maybe they decided to sell the books to someone else," John said.

"I hope not," Claire replied.

"What do we do now?" Rachel asked.

"Wait and see if we hear from them again," Claire said. "What else can we do?"

"I have to get back to the university," said Rachel. "If the seller does show up, find a way to keep 'em here and call me."

"Will do," said John.

Rachel pulled her hair out of the bun, shook the powder out, hooked the backpack over her shoulders, and dropped about thirty years.

"You doing anything for lunch?" John asked Claire once Rachel had left.

"No."

"I can't leave the store, but I'll treat if you'll go over to Woody's and get some sandwiches."

Claire came back with two turkey and green chile on rye. John left a message at the counter to call him if anyone showed up. They went to the conference room, shut the door, and ate their lunch. Claire had been thinking about the books while she waited in the bathroom, finding *The History of the Blue* to be conspicuous by its absence from the e-mail list. She could understand why a thief would hold onto the folio, but why keep the history?

"It's not worth selling," John said when she mentioned it.

"How would a thief know that? It was in a box marked valuable books."

"A thief might not, but a book dealer would," said John.

Claire thought of John and Rachel as terriers holding tight to the bones of their suspects. John was convinced the thief was a dealer. Rachel was equally convinced it was a librarian. Claire was open to the possibility that it was someone else, although the other prospects were also unpleasing to contemplate. "Where is your copy?" she asked John.

"On the Southwest shelf."

Claire finished her sandwich and went to the Southwest section to look. The space where deWitt's *History of the Blue* should have been was empty. The adjacent books tilted to one side as if they were trying to fill a void. John followed Claire and peered over her shoulder.

"It's gone," she said.

"So it is," he agreed.

"Are you sure you didn't sell it?"

"Pretty sure," said John. He went to his office, checked the inventory on the computer, and found the history listed as being in stock. The publisher was High Plains Press in Las Vegas, New Mexico.

"It could have been stolen," Claire said. This was a store, after all, whose security system consisted of a couple of mirrors mounted on the wall.

"Or sold by someone who forgot to enter it on the computer." John shrugged.

"If it turns up, will you let me know?"

"Sure," said John.

Claire had left herself the option of taking the entire day off, but she had work to do and returned to her office, where she found a voice-mail message saying that Rachel had called.

Rachel surprised her by actually answering her phone. "You're disappointed, aren't you?" she asked.

"Yes. "

"Me, too. We kept an eye on the library's parking lot and noticed that three of your coworkers were absent at the time set for the sting."

"Who?"

"Harrison Hough, Ruth O'Connor, and Gail Benton. We didn't have the resources to follow them, so all we know is that none of them showed up at Page One, Too. You might be able to do a little investigating of your own to find out where they went."

"I'll try," Claire said. But first she logged onto her computer, looked up the call number for the library's copy of *The History of the Blue,* and discovered it had been shelved in the tower. On her way she passed Harrison's office and poked her head in the door.

"How was the *Songs of the Cowboys*?" he asked her.

"Not good. It smelled moldy and had water stains. The red of the cover had bled onto the pages. Overall, it was in very poor condition." Some renegade part of her relished embellishing her lie.

"Pity. That's a book I'd like to add to our collection."

"How was your day?"

"Fine. I went to a Friends of the Library luncheon."

"By yourself?"

"Ruth came along. She's good at dealing with the friends." Harrison looked down at the papers on his desk, indicating that Claire's allotted time was over.

While she waited for the elevator to the tower, Claire recalled what she'd heard about the series of thefts that took place here several years ago. The thief, a notorious con artist, brought the books out

106

on the dumbwaiter and handed them to his wife, who hid them under her dress pretending to be pregnant. The library responded by sealing off the dumbwaiter and making it impossible to use the elevator without punching in a security code. The tower was now limited to books from the center's collection and, in theory anyway, could only be accessed by people who worked here. If a student wanted a book, a librarian had to retrieve it.

The thief was imaginative and skilled at manufacturing artifacts, such as Billy the Kid's belt buckle or the tablets the Phoenicians left behind when they sailed up the Rio Grande. Even more remarkable was the fact that he persuaded people to buy them. When the FBI raided his house, it was filled with skulls and pots the con artist had either created or dug up. It took an archaeologist and forensic anthropologist to tell the difference. The con artist served a short prison sentence, then became a used-car salesman, where Claire suspected he was applying his imagination and skills to another dubious purpose.

She punched in her code, the elevator arrived, and she rode it to the fifth floor. Claire found the tower to be an ambivalent place, but it made some of her coworkers so uncomfortable they refused to go there. From the outside it was inspiring, a nice counterpoint to the squat library, but inside it could be onimous. When the wind blew, it whistled through cracks in the windows. Lights were known to flicker and dim. As soon as the electricity went on in one part of the building, it went off in another. It was rare to run into anyone in the tower, and Claire had a sense of apprehension whenever she did. The windows looking out over the campus reminded her of the sniper who fired on students at the University of Texas or the bell tower Kim Novak jumped from in *Vertigo*. She was always prepared for something strange to happen in the tower, although nothing ever had.

She circled the fifth floor quickly and saw that no one was there, but someone had been. A pile of papers that had been assembled by a pack rat or a librarian sat on a table in a carrel. As Claire walked through the stacks, following call numbers to the spot where *The History of the Blue* was supposed to be, she heard the elevator creaking its way up the shaft. The tower was designed for storage, not comfort. There were no interior walls, and the space was broken up only by metal bookshelves. The floors were thin. Sound reverberated throughout the tower, and often it was impossible to tell exactly where the sound was coming from. Footsteps might be above or below. In this environment, sounds provoked strange associations. The creaking elevator made Claire think of a student who had been decapitated by an elevator in another UNM building. She listened to the door slide open and shut, causing the lights to flicker as it did. From the sound of it, she couldn't tell whether the elevator had stopped at her floor or another, and she waited for footsteps to reveal whether she was sharing this floor with someone else. When she heard nothing, she called out, "Hello?" The only answer was the elevator rumbling back down the shaft.

She peered around the corner, saw no one by the elevator door, and resumed her search for *The History of the Blue*. Possibly somebody had pressed the number for a particular floor, had been diverted, and had gotten off the elevator before it began its ascent. As Claire walked down the aisle between the shelves, she heard the sound of footsteps echoing her own. When she walked, other feet walked. When she stopped, they stopped. When she turned, they turned. For a minute she had the sensation a ghost had stepped out of one of the history books that surrounded her. "You're being ridiculous," she said to herself, but when she continued walking, she heard the footsteps again. There might be someone on the floor above, following her in an attempt to ascertain what she was looking for or to intimidate. She could also be hearing her own footsteps echoing somewhere else in the building.

Claire reached the place where the history should have been shelved, but not wanting to reveal her purpose, she walked by it without stopping, glancing at the spot only long enough to see a hole in the sequence of numbers. Stolen? she wondered, or—the bane of libraries—mis-shelved? It would have been easy enough for a librarian to have taken it or moved it. Harder, but not impossible, for someone else. She continued walking through the stacks, stopping a few minutes later in front of another book and listening as she took it from the shelf. She waited, heard nothing, then walked back to the elevator. Had there been any footsteps, she wondered? Or had the sound been the result of an overactive imagination and a stressful day? Claire pressed the elevator button, drumming her fingers against the wall while she waited for it to reach her floor. The lights flickered when the door opened. In the dimness inside the elevator, the shadow she saw was her own.

CHAPTER NINE

Claire worked late that night, hunched over her computer while one by one her coworkers passed by on their way home. When she was sure everyone had left, she walked down the hall to Gail's office. The lights were off, and the computer screen was dark. If Gail had turned the computer off, Claire wouldn't have been able to log onto it without a password. It was possible the screen was programmed to shut off after a period of inactivity as Claire's was. She put her hand on the mouse and slid it across the pad. The screen lit up with the Windows icons illuminating the dirty mugs, the scattered papers, the mess that was Gail's desk. Claire found the place where Gail kept track of her appointments. For today, Thursday, at noon, Gail had entered, "Doctor's appointment. Ask about P." She skimmed through the next couple of days and saw that on Friday Gail had scheduled a lunch with Claire's predecessor, Irina. She logged out of the computer and left Gail's office. She might have discovered more by checking other dates, but she didn't want to linger and take the risk of getting caught or to invade Gail's privacy any more than she had to.

Driving home along Tramway she wondered if P could be Percocet, a large white pill like the one she'd seen Gail swallowing and a painkiller Claire had taken once following surgery. She remembered the feeling of lying in bed and letting the drug turn her muscles to silk. It was a smooth, elegant feeling, too smooth to be good for you, and when the prescription ran out, Claire didn't renew it. Percocet was addictive and being on it could explain Gail's erratic behavior.

When Claire got home, she cooked herself a Poor Melissa pasta dinner and went to bed early. In the middle of the night, she had an erotic dream involving, of all people, her ex-husband. She woke up feeling sated but annoyed with him for having invaded her sleep. How long would it be, she wondered, before she was free of Evan? Light from a streetlamp silhouetted the bare branches of a neighbor's elm tree against her wall, turning them into a map of meandering rivers and roads. Wanting to escape from thoughts of Evan, Claire let her mind take a less familiar journey into the labyrinth of the criminal mind, a place that intrigued her more than she ever would have expected. She'd been surprised by how easily and well she had lied. She suspected the rush it induced could become as addictive as a drug. The key to continuing the behavior but avoiding the addiction was self-control and moderation—indulging rarely and only when necessary.

She replayed the events of the day. Although she'd been hoping for resolution at Page One, Too, all she'd gotten were a few weak leads. Was the fact that Harrison and Ruth had an engagement proof that neither was the thief or merely an indication that their plans had changed? Had Gail really had a doctor's appointment? Or was that entry a lie and P the detail that gave it credence? Could she have been headed for Page One, Too and gotten spooked at the last minute? Why was she having lunch with Irina? Where was Irina living, and what was she doing? Did the missing copies of *The History of the Blue* signify anything? Shelving was not an exact science. Claire knew she could have chosen another book at random and had the same outcome. She wondered if Irina still had access to the tower. Could she or Gail or anyone else have shadowed her from another floor as she walked through the stacks? As Claire fell back asleep, her thoughts lead to I-25, the road to Las Vegas and High Plains Press.

The next day she called Lola Falter several times. When she didn't get an answer, she tried her friend, Madelyn, at the U of A.

"How's the book quest going?" Madelyn asked. "I haven't heard anything about them here."

"Someone offered to sell most of the missing books to John Harlan at Page One, Too anonymously over the Internet," Claire replied. "We arranged a sting operation with a university policewoman, but the seller never showed up."

"Would you bring those books to John Harlan, if you were the thief?"

"No, but Rachel, the policewoman, tells me it's hard to underestimate the intelligence of the average thief."

"This may not be your average thief."

"True. Whoever it is didn't offer John the Austin/Adams folio."

"I'd be looking on the art market for the prints."

"*The History of the Blue* that was in my box wasn't offered, either."

"Do you care about that book? It's not worth anything."

"It's missing from John's shelves and from the stacks here, which is strange. Maybe somebody wants it for its content rather than the size of its first printing or its collectibility."

"Value a book for its content? Now, that would be rare."

"It was printed by High Plains Press in Las Vegas. I've been calling Lola Falter there, but not getting any answer or an answering machine, either."

"Lola's pretty old. She closed the press down years ago, but as far as I know, she still lives in Las Vegas. Do you want me to see if I can locate our copy of the history?"

"Please."

Madelyn called back later. "The online catalog said to check the shelf, but it wasn't there. As you know, it's not unusual for books to disappear. There are people who consider libraries to be payment optional bookstores."

"So I've been told."

"Say hello to Lola when you find her."

"Will do."

The Eliot Porter photos had been matted, framed, and stacked in the tower waiting to be hung in the exhibition room. Whenever she had a free moment, Claire looked through them, savoring their beauty and taking pride in her part in the exhibit. Harrison had agreed to have a punch and chips reception at the opening. While Claire was making up the invitation list, the idea occurred to her to invite Irina. She didn't know if Irina would consider returning to the center or even if she was still in town, but Claire was curious about her predecessor. She'd been wanting to broach the subject of Irina with Gail, and this gave her the opportunity.

She walked down the hall to Gail's office with the address list in her hand, and found Gail working on her computer. "I was wondering if you knew how to reach Irina," Claire said.

"Why do you want to get in touch with her?"

"I was thinking of inviting her to the Eliot Porter reception."

Gail laughed. "She won't come."

"Why not?"

"She hates the library. After all she contributed to this place, she was denied tenure. How would that make you feel?"

"Not good. Does she ever come back?"

"Not if she can help it."

"What's she doing? Is she still in Albuquerque? Did she find another job?"

"Another job in Albuquerque?" Gail raised a pair of dubious eyebrows. They both knew this was a one-university town. "She's still here, but she is looking elsewhere."

"What is she doing in the meantime?"

"Writing a novel."

In Claire's mind that was a one-way ticket to poverty.

She woke up Saturday morning feeling the lure of the open highway. She'd been spending too much time indoors staring at a computer screen. She tried Lola Falter once again and got a busy signal, but when she called back fifteen minutes later, there was no answer. Claire decided to go to Las Vegas to see if she could find Lola. It was a hundred-and-twenty-mile drive, which would be a long, tense trip on either coast, but was a pleasant experience here on a section of I-25 that had a lot of distant blue mountains and a minimum of large trucks. She could give her Chevy free rein and let it reach a cruising speed of eighty miles an hour.

Las Vegas was a town that was always on the verge of being discovered, but had never crossed the line. For years Claire had been hearing that it would be the next Santa Fe, but it was still the old Las Vegas and she admired it for that. It was a town that had sprung up along the railroad, full of charming Victorian houses, a sleepy plaza, and a couple of rambling hotels. Every year or so one art gallery opened and another one closed. Claire wondered why it had never developed as an art colony; it had the location, it had the beauty. But it also had a fierce wind that spun dust devils down the street, that rattled your windows and your brain, making it impossible to think. It could be hard to create with the wind blowing grit through your head.

Claire stopped at the ice-cream parlor on Main Street for lunch. It was a building she loved, with a high tin ceiling and gingerbread balcony that would be a great place to store books. She had a BLT on white toast and an ice-cream soda. Then she went looking for Lola Falter.

Lola lived in a tiny Victorian house that had a peaked roof covered with cedar shakes. It had once been painted lavender, but had faded to the color of old lingerie. A sign that read HIGH PLAINS PRESS in purple letters flapped in the breeze. High Plains had occasionally published a collection of poetry or a regional novel, but mostly it was a vanity press. Although authors paid Lola to publish their books, she put her heart in it. Sometimes the content was obscure, but High Plains Press books were always beautiful to look at and a pleasure to hold.

Claire pushed the doorbell, a button protruding from the back of a rusty lizard, and heard the bell chiming somewhere inside the house. She waited, heard no movement, and pushed the bell again. "Coming," Lola called out, but it took her so long to get to the door, Claire began to think she had imagined the sound of Lola's voice. It was easy to imagine voices in the wind. While she waited, the wind picked up a black garbage bag, blew it down the street, and impaled it on Lola's picket fence, turning it into a flapping raven. Claire began to turn away when the door opened, and Lola stood before her, bracing herself against the bars of a walker.

The last time Claire saw her, she was standing tall and walking unassisted. Stifling the impulse to blurt out "I'm sorry," Claire said only, "Hello, Lola."

"Claire Reynier," Lola replied. "What are you doing in Las Vegas?"

"I came to see you. I've been calling, but I never get an answer."

"It takes me so long to get to the phone these days, a lot of people just hang up. Most of the time that's all right with me." Lola focused her sharp black eyes on Claire. "Did you come all the way from Tucson?"

"I live in Albuquerque now."

"Come on in. Tell me what's on your mind."

Claire followed while Lola made her way down the hall, scooting like a crab from one side of the walker to the other. Lola went into a tiny living room and lowered herself into a recliner, motioning Claire into a deep and dusty armchair. Once she was out of the walker, Lola looked more like the person Claire knew. She had a thin face with a hooked nose and a shock of white hair. Her eyes were lively and bright. Claire remembered her father's comment that when a person aged, either the body went or the mind. To Lola, the mind would be more important than the body.

"What are you doing in Albuquerque?" Lola asked.

"Working at the Center for Southwest Research."

"I was sorry to hear about Burke's death."

"That's part of the reason I'm here." Claire told Lola about the theft and the missing *History of the Blue.*

"When did I publish that book anyway?" Lola asked herself. "Seventy-two? Seventy-three? There weren't very many of them as I recall. See that filing cabinet in the dining room? Take a look, please, and see if you can find a file for deWitt."

Lola's oak filing cabinet was jam-packed with files—thirty years worth—but High Plains Press had only published three or four books a year in its heyday and hadn't published anything at all for several years. Claire found deWitt's manila folder in the *d*'s where it belonged, pulled it out, and took it to Lola, who brushed the dust off and opened it up.

"I published thirty copies," Lola said. "DeWitt wanted it to go to local libraries, historical societies, and members of the family."

Claire knew that if Lola published it, she had read it and might well remember what it said. "What was in it? Was there information anyone might want to steal the book for?"

"You mean maps of buried treasure or the answer to who killed Arthur Manby?" The Manby murder was one of the great unsolved crimes of the Southwest.

"I don't know. It's odd that so many of them have disappeared."

"As I remember, it was just a nice little history of the Blue. Who settled where when, who married who, who begat who. DeWitt died before the book came out, and Burke made all the publishing arrangements. I have an invoice here that he paid." The phone rang, but Lola made no attempt to get out of her chair.

"Do you want me to answer it?" Claire asked.

"No. It'll just be somebody trying to sell me something. They think because I'm an old lady, I'm an easy mark."

"You'll never be an easy mark."

"I would hope not." The phone rang a perfunctory four times and stopped. "Burke picked the history up. He said he was going to distribute the books as Ben requested, and I assume he did."

"We had one, the U of A had one, John Harlan had one, but they're all gone. Do you have a copy here?"

"Not anymore. I've been getting rid of things. It's that time of life, you know?"

Claire did know, but Lola's mind had been so focused and clear while they talked that she had temporarily forgotten what the walker indicated.

"I gave my copy to the local library a couple of years ago."

"I'll try there."

"Could I get you a cup of tea or anything?"

Claire said no. Lola's energy seemed to be fading, and she didn't want to watch her struggling to get out of the chair. "Your High Plains Press records would be very valuable to the center, Lola."

"Really? Do you think anybody will be interested?"

"I think a lot of people would be interested."

"Would you like me to get them together for you?"

"Yes, but there's no rush. Whenever it's convenient."

Lola's hand gripped the arm of her chair, and she started to pull herself forward. Claire put her hand over Lola's. "Don't get up. I'll let myself out and lock the door behind me."

"It was good to see you, Claire," Lola said.

"My pleasure," Claire replied.

She drove to the library, which had been donated to the town of Las Vegas by the capitalist/philanthropist Andrew Carnegie, who, in Claire's opinion, was a contemptible human being. He would lock the unions out of his factories and let the workers starve before he'd pay them another nickel. His vast profits had been made on the backs and the souls of his workers. He screwed his business partners and left a trail of human wreckage behind him, but he also left a string of magnificent libraries. Small towns and cities all across the country felt the results of Carnegie's beneficence. Could it really be beneficence, Claire wondered, if the impulse to give came from atonement? Was that generosity or blood money?

Whatever the cause, the Andrew Carnegie Library in Las Vegas, was a wonderful building. Long after the Carnegie controversy was over and the people involved in it were dead, the library went on providing shelter and encouraging people to read. Having already found three empty slots on three shelves, Claire was apprehensive about locating the history. Nevertheless, she looked up the call number on the computer and went searching for it among the shelves, only to find another empty space.

A librarian was sitting at a desk, working on a computer. Her head was bent, and the overhead light brought out the black sheen of her hair. Claire stood in front of the desk and waited until the librarian had finished typing out her sentence. When the woman looked up and acknowledged her presence, Claire introduced herself.

"I'm Claire Reynier. I'm in charge of collection development at the Center for Southwest Research at UNM."

"Yes?" the woman asked. Her name, Rosa Martinez, was printed on a plaque sitting on her desk, and she didn't repeat it. Rosa was a small person with large eyes and quick movements. Claire didn't know what kind of reaction to expect from her. Sometimes being a UNM librarian inspired respect, sometimes hostility; in some circles university people were considered arrogant, as John Harlan liked to remind her. It wasn't often that Claire encountered indifference, but that appeared to be Rosa's attitude.

Her fingers hovered over her keyboard, making it clear that Claire's time was limited, and she got right to the point. "I've been looking for Benjamin deWitt's *The History of the Blue* printed by High Plains Press. It's not on the shelf." Claire expected a shrug and a comment about the vicissitudes of mis-shelving.

But Rosa turned her attention away from the computer screen and into the archives of her mind. Her fingers drummed the edge of the keyboard while she thought.

"Could it have been stolen?" Claire asked.

"No. We had a library sale last year and got rid of a lot of those regional histories," she said. "We haven't updated the computer yet to reflect the sale, but as I remember, the deWitt book was one of the ones we sold. Do you know Anthony Barbour?"

"Yes," Claire replied. Anthony was an itinerant book scout who made a living, more or less, by picking up a book at places where it wasn't appreciated—garage sales, library sales, estate sales—and taking it someplace it would be, then selling it to make a quick buck.

"I'd give him a try," Rosa said. "He was here for the sale, and I know he has customers who collect small-town histories. Would you like his number?"

"I have it." In Claire's card file, there was a business card that read "Anthony Barbour, Vagabond Book Scout. Have books. Will travel." "But that doesn't necessarily get you Anthony."

"Leave a message," Rosa said. "Sooner or later he'll show up or call you back." She looked back at her computer screen. "Anything else?"

"Have you read *The History of the Blue*?"

"No." Rosa shook her head.

"Thanks for your help."

Rosa had started typing again. "Glad to do it. Good luck," she said.

On the drive back to Albuquerque, Claire thought about Anthony and his vagabond life. A man in his mid-thirties, he lived like a sixties hippie driving a VW van that was twenty-five years old at least. Anthony was happiest on the road, and even during the time he had been married, he'd always spent a lot of time there. It was rumored that he came home unexpectedly one day to find his wife in bed with another man, and after that the van became his home. Anthony shared Claire's love of books and maps, and a visit from him was always a good way to spend an afternoon.

When she got home, she called him and got a recording of Willie Nelson singing, "On the Road Again." She left a message on his machine, which resembled putting a note in a bottle and tossing it into the ocean. Claire knew that it could be awhile before Anthony called her back, but she also knew that once he got her message, he wouldn't sell the history to anyone else.

CHAPTER TEN

Anthony's footloose lifestyle had a certain appeal when the alarm went off Monday morning, announcing that Claire had to get to the library. There were catalogs to read, coworkers to deal with, and a message to answer from Sally Froelich.

"I heard from Walter Massey," Sally said when Claire returned the call.

Claire took a large sip from her coffee. "What does he want?"

"To set up a meeting with his clients, who, as you know, are not happy with the will. You need to be there; you know better than anyone what Burke intended and whether there is any possibility of coming to terms with the heirs."

"All right," Claire sighed. "Set it up."

The meeting was arranged for Friday in Massey's office on the grounds that his location was more convenient for everyone, including Claire, since it was close to the interstate and the university. Claire suspected that the real reason Massey wanted to have the meeting in his office was that it would give him more control and put him in a better bargaining position, but she agreed, saving her energy for what she felt was the important battle—honoring the terms of Burke's will.

Massey's office was in a strip mall. His conference room had gold shag carpeting on the floor and fake wood paneling on the walls. All it needed to make it a male bonding den was a TV screen displaying the Denver Broncos and a coffee table overflowing with chips and beer. There was a conference table big enough to play pool on. The plastic blinds on the windows were open to reveal a view of the parking lot. Claire arrived on time and found Massey's clients lined up at the conference table, suggesting that they'd already had a meeting. Corinne was absent, which didn't surprise Claire. She hated to leave the ranch, and Claire wasn't convinced she was committed to the purpose of this meeting. James and Laura were at the table, wearing matching navy blue leisure suits. Laura looked crisp and efficient with every strand of her blonde hair in place. Every strand of James's comb-over was in place, too, but he slouched in his chair. His body language was tired and defeated. Or was it repressed? Claire wondered. The spark was gone from the James she once knew.

Samantha's hair was carefully tousled, and she wore a jacket woven into the pattern of a Navajo rug. She was sitting beside a man Claire didn't recognize. His coarse red hair was pulled back into a ponytail. He had a thin, bony face and a sharp nose. His hazel eyes had an amused expression that appeared to have been perfected by practice. His lips were too soft and full for the rest of his face. He wore painter's pants and two T-shirts, a faded red one with tears strategically placed so the faded blue of his under T showed through. Samantha introduced him as Rusty Siler, and Claire recalled this was the artist she had mentioned she was involved with. He was not a party to the will, and Claire felt he had no business being at the meeting unless he and Samantha had gotten married. She glanced at the hands on the table, not seeing any wedding rings, and noticed that Rusty Siler's fingers were stained with paint.

Massey entered the conference room, greeting everyone like an obsequious host. Claire recoiled at his overbearing manner, but his arrival kept her from having to make small talk with the heirs. Sally arrived a few minutes later, complaining about the traffic on Central. She wore a voluminous cotton dress, and a silver ear cuff hugged her ear. Massey sat down at the head of the table. Sally and

Claire sat on the side across from Burke's offspring and their significant others.

Massey made his opening remarks. How was everybody? Did everybody know everybody? Their purpose for being here was to discuss the terms of Burke's will, to make sure that everyone was treated fairly, that the family was taken care of, that Burke's wishes were followed, that differences were settled amicably. Claire began to wish Sally had insisted on having the meeting in her office. The extra ten minutes driving time would have been worth it. Sally's office was gracious and comfortable. People wouldn't be slamming car doors and arguing outside the window. To discuss rare and valuable things would have made more sense in an atmosphere where they were appreciated.

While Massey droned on, an underlying annoyance Claire had been feeling about Burke surfaced. Why hadn't he foreseen that the terms of the will would cause trouble? Why had he given her this responsibility? She loved him and admired him, but his irascibility could be annoying. Her eyes looked out the window and focused on a patch of blue sky visible above the parking lot. Massey cleared his throat, opened the file he'd placed on the table, and got to the point.

"It is our belief that Burke Lovell was incapacitated and the victim of undue influence at the time the will was signed," he said.

Claire had already been over this weary ground with Massey. "That's not true," she replied.

"We have in our possession a signed affidavit from the witness Kassandra Wells."

"We're aware of that," Sally said.

He reached into his file and pulled out his ace. "Now we have one from the second witness, Jed Acker."

The family members stared out the window or down at the table, but Rusty Siler looked up and smiled at Claire without opening his soft, full lips.

"I'd like to see that affidavit," said Sally. Massey handed it over. Sally read it and passed it along to Claire, who studied the document with a sick feeling. "Just how did you get Jed to sign that?" Sally asked.

"He volunteered." Massey hunched his vulture shoulders and hovered over the table. "That's two out of the three people who were with Lovell at the time the will was signed. And the two who say he was incompetent were witnesses."

"If they thought he was incompetent, why did they sign?" Sally asked. "I would say that witnessing a will implies competency."

"Or coercion," Massey replied.

"Coercion!" Sally jeered. "What coercion? Did Burke or Claire hold a gun to the witnesses heads?"

"He was their boss."

"Oh, please," replied Sally.

Massey continued down this slippery path. "Claire is the only one who claims Burke was competent at the time the will was signed, and Claire has a vested interest." He had begun talking about Claire as if she weren't in the room, focusing his eyes on Sally as he spoke.

He lacks the courage to face me, Claire thought, because he knows what he's saying is a lie. She had been letting Sally do the talking, but Massey tried her patience. "And what is my vested interest?" she inquired.

"He left his rare-book collection to you," Massey said.

"He didn't leave it to me. He left it to the library. Has anyone else here expressed the slightest interest in Burke's book collection?"

James studied his hands. Laura smoothed her hair. Samantha looked out the window, seemingly fascinated by a car that was pulling out of a parking space. Only Rusty Siler looked at Claire with amusement in his eyes.

Massey changed his tactic, focusing on Claire and saying in a coaxing tone. "You hadn't seen Burke in a while. Is there any possibility you misread his mental state?"

"No," Claire replied, digging in her heels.

"Do we have anything else to discuss here?" Sally asked, making a show of looking at her watch.

"We intend to file a petition to prevent probate under the law of undue influence or incapacity," Massey said.

Sally looked across the table at the family members. "You can spend all your inheritance fighting the will," she said. "Then the principal beneficiary of Burke P. Lovell's estate will be"—she turned toward Massey—"your lawyer."

"You are well aware that a lawyer does not speak directly to another lawyer's clients," Massey said.

Sally shifted her weight in her chair, faced him, and said, "All right, then, I'll say it to you. You are involving your clients in a frivolous and unnecessary lawsuit. Win or lose, your legal fees will take up most of what they stand to gain from their inheritance."

"There is also the issue of paternity," Massey continued.

"Whose paternity?"

"Mariah Geraty's."

Sally nodded to Claire to say forewarned is forearmed. "It's a nonissue. The will says the ranch goes to Mariah Geraty, not Burke's daughter Mariah Geraty."

"It is an issue if Mariah Geraty deceived Lovell."

"The burden of proving that is on you." With the rudeness that comes naturally to lawyers, she stood up, looked at her beeper, and indicated that the meeting was over. "Can I use your phone? I have to make a call."

"Be my guest," Massey said, indicating a phone on a table in the corner. He excused himself to make a phone call of his own.

Claire was left at the table with the heirs while the lawyers conducted their other business. "Have you given any thought to the books you'd like?" she asked Samantha and James.

"No," said James.

"There must be *something* you want," Laura said.

"No, nothing." James got up from the table, walked to the window, and stared out.

"I've been too busy," said Samantha.

"Samantha told me that you work at the Center for Southwest Research," Rusty Siler said to Claire.

"That's right."

"I read in the *Reporter* that the center is exhibiting some Eliot Porter photos that have never been shown."

"We are."

"Which ones?"

"The violets in Appalachia, the canyon lands of Utah, the apple trees in Tesuque."

"The Appalachian violets was a favorite of Eliot's."

"Oh?"

"I had a studio in Tesuque, and we were neighbors. I was good friends with Eliot and his wife," he said, name-dropping in Santa Fe style.

"We're having an opening for the photographs in the exhibition hall Friday night. You might like to come."

"We'd love to," said Samantha, hooking her arm in Rusty's, "but we have other plans."

"We'll try to make it," said Rusty.

"Ready?" asked the no-nonsense Sally, who had completed her phone call.

"Ready," Claire replied.

"I'll walk you to your car," Sally said. "What was that guy doing with Samantha?" she asked as soon as they were out the door.

"He's her boyfriend, an artist named Rusty Siler."

"From Santa Fe?"

"Yes."

"Never heard of him," Sally said, dismissing Rusty Siler. She was an art collector who made it her business to know who was hot, who was up-and-coming, who was neither. "Did I hear him tell you he was Eliot Porter's neighbor in Tesuque? Gardener would be more like it," she snorted.

They reached Sally's car, a silver Lexus, and stopped beside it. "You know, there was a lot of bullshit and bluffing going on in there," she said, "but the truth is with both witnesses now willing to testify that Burke was incompetent, Massey has an excellent case. What I said about legal fees eating up the inheritance applies to both sides. I'm not her lawyer, but I believe it would be in Mariah's best interests to discuss a settlement. Can you talk to her?"

"I'll try."

"Have you heard anything yet from the Genealogical Search Company?"

"No."

"I'd give them a call."

"Will do."

"Good luck," said Sally.

Claire prepared herself a cup of tea and called the Genealogical Search Company when she got back to her office. "We're just about finished with our report," Joe Hopper said. "We found the birth certificate for Mariah Geraty, and it doesn't list a father."

"The copy I have lists Burke P. Lovell."

"His name must have been added later, possibly with an attempt to defraud."

"Wouldn't that depend on whether the person who added it was the father or not?"

"True," said Joe Hopper. "The best way to establish that would be through DNA testing. We found no record of who Mariah Geraty's father is and no record of any previously unacknowledged off-spring or heirs for Burke Lovell. We'll get the report in the mail to you."

"Thanks," Claire replied.

She knew this information would mean another trip back to the Blue, but the Porter reception was scheduled for Friday and she decided to put the trip on hold until the reception was over.

She examined the copy of Mariah's birth certificate she had on file. It looked as if it had been copied on one of those second-rate Xerox machines located in libraries and drugstores. Put in a dime, and they spit out a copy, but not a very good copy. The letters on this copy were blurred around the edges. She looked into the rectangle that held the father's name. The letters in Burke P. Lovell were as dark as the other entries, suggesting they had been typed on the same machine at the same time, but on closer examination, she could see that the typeface was different. The tail was clipped on the *l*'s, and the vowels were rounder. Claire had experience authenticating documents, and was annoyed that she hadn't scrutinized this one more carefully. Too much stress, she thought, too little time. She called Sally to tell her what she had discovered.

"Could the forger be Mariah?" Sally asked.

"That's what I'll have to find out."

"How do you intend to do it?"

"Ask her."

"It might work," Sally said.

That afternoon Claire left work early and went for a walk in Elena Gallegos Park in the foothills. The park spanned several life zones beginning at the 6,000 foot elevation, which was scattered with cholla and prickly pear, and ending at 10,000 feet in a conifer and aspen forest. Claire walked toward the mountains as far as the wilderness gate, then she turned back, stopping at a monument to an environmentalist who had helped design the park and who had died young in a climbing accident. The monument was a series of sculpted boulders that stood like sentinels in the desert, in formation, but also very much alone. This late in the day the stones cast long shadows. The silence and solitude of the monument spoke to Claire's dark moods. She visualized the boulders as tombstones, tributes to the men who had departed her life: Burke, her father, even Evan, who was dead to her now. The Porter exhibit was coming up, her job was challenging, her life was moving forward in a positive way. But in order to move forward, sometimes it was necessary to go back and touch base with the past. While Claire thought about Burke and all she had lost, the shadows deepened and the sun sank behind the West Mesa, turning the lingering jet trails to gold.

The Porter reception went well. The exhibition room was packed. Most of the people Claire had invited came: booksellers, writers, art historians. Sally Froelich and John Harlan were there. The library staff made an appearance. Rex Barker drove up from Socorro. Claire didn't have time to look at the photographs, but she could feel them shimmering on the exhibition room's walls. Snatches of praise floated around the room like bubbles. She tried to reach out and grab them, but Harrison got in the way.

"Thank you," she heard him say while he held court in the middle of the room, playing the part of gracious host in his navy blazer and turtleneck. "To be sure, I am extremely proud of these prints. It is an honor for me to be able to exhibit them here."

I? Claire thought, Me? remembering how Harrison had resisted *her* idea. John Harlan came up and offered her a cup of punch. "Hey, Claire," he said in his Texas twang. "You sure have done a great job here." Claire felt she'd been handed sparkling wine instead of a punch that was duller than dishwater. "But that pompous poobah is taking all the credit."

"That's the way he is," Claire said, attempting to shrug Harrison off.

John made a show of turning his head and looking behind his shoulder.

"What are you doing?" Claire asked.

"Just wanted to make sure no one was preparing to stab me in the back. Can't be too careful here in the land of the kiss ass and the suck up. You know, Claire, you ought to consider coming to work for me and gettin' away from this place."

"On what you'd pay me, I'd have to live in a tepee."

John had always lived in dark apartments full of books, never considering there could be anything better. "You could . . ."

He didn't get to finish his sentence, because Ruth O'Connor walked up and inserted a comma into the conversation. "Harrison might have spent some more money on the refreshments," she said, eyeing her punch with disdain.

"He's the kind of guy who'd drive to Socorro to save a dime," John replied.

"Speaking of Socorro," Ruth replied. "Rex Barker knows how to work a room."

Rex was talking to a young woman with chestnut hair tumbling down her back. Claire noticed that not far away Gail was alone leaning against the wall. She'd been looking for an opportunity to talk to Gail, so she excused herself to John and Ruth and walked over. Claire had dressed up for this occasion, as much as anyone ever did in Albuquerque, in a black dress and a silver Navajo pin from the thirties that had belonged to her mother. Gail was in a drab gray dress and slouching like she was trying to disappear.

"Nice exhibit," Gail said, which was the best she was able to do and about as much as Claire expected.

Claire knew most of the people here, but not all. "Did Irina come?" she asked. Ignoring Gail's advice, Claire had sent out the invitation. She had no idea what Irina looked like, and didn't know if she was in the room or not.

"No," Gail replied.

"I'm sorry. I was hoping to meet her."

Gail shrugged. "I told you she would never come back here, didn't I? Excuse me."

She walked away, and Claire watched her weave through the crowd, wondering if she might have been drinking something other than punch.

John Harlan was back at her elbow. "Claire, I've been wantin' to ask you if . . ."

"Hey," Rex Barker said over Claire's shoulder. How could someone so tall arrive so unexpectedly? she wondered. His black jeans, black shirt, and black cowboy hat made him seem even taller. Rex was like a shadow. When he moved straight on, you saw him; when he moved sideways, he disappeared.

"Hey," said John Harlan.

"Hello, Rex," Claire said. She was surprised he had come. Rex wasn't very good at small talk, and he avoided parties.

John started talking to someone he knew, and Claire felt Rex edging his way between them, as if he were trying to cut her out of the herd. When his back was to John, he leaned over and said, "Could I talk to you alone?"

"When?"

"Now?" he asked, surprising Claire by his intensity.

She looked around, saw that people were starting to leave, and led Rex down the hall to her office.

"Being at a party makes me nervous as a cat in a roomful of

rocking chairs," he said, shaking his shoulders as if he was shaking off a bad dream.

Claire turned on her desk lamp. The hallway was dark, and the light created a feeling of intimacy, a circle isolating her and Rex from everyone else. The party at the other end of the hallway seemed very far away.

Rex took off his hat and laid it on the desk. His black hair had begun graying at the temples. He had gaunt cheeks and hooded turtle eyes that served him well in poker and in bed. Unsociable as he was, there were women who found Rex Barker irresistible. Years ago he had published a collection of romantic poems about an older woman he claimed he'd been passionately in love with. The woman died. There were no witnesses left to prove or disprove the claim, but Claire had never known Rex to be passionate about anything other than poker and cigarettes. As far as she knew, Rex hadn't written a word since, but he continued to cash in with women on the lonely writer mystique he'd created with his poetry book.

Rex took a pack of Camels from his pocket and pulled out a cigarette. "Mind if I smoke?"

Claire shook her head. "You can't in here."

Rex looked at the dark hallway, then bent his head toward Claire as if they were conspirators. He rolled the unlit cigarette in his fingers, and Claire noticed that he wore a silver watch band and a large turquoise ring.

"I got an offer to sell your books," he said in a stage whisper. "The novels anyway."

"From who?"

"I don't know. It came over the Internet from anon.net.fi, that's a server that forwards mail anonymously."

"I'm aware of that."

"What do you want me to do about it?"

"Buy them," Claire said.

"We're looking at twelve thousand dollars here if I buy them as a dealer. Eighteen if I buy them as a collector. I don't have that kind of money." Rex put his cigarette in his mouth, remembered it was unlit, and took it out.

"I'll cover it. Can you get the seller to bring the books to you so you can look them over to make sure they're the library's books, and we can find out who the seller is?"

"I doubt it. He says he'll only deal by mail. He ships the books to me. I get a chance to look at them. If I like them, I pay the shipper by a cashier's check made out to cash."

"Which shipper?"

"He won't say."

"Do you know it's a he?"

Rex tapped his cigarette against Claire's desk. "Not really."

"The trouble with this plan is we may never find out who the seller is."

Rex's eyelids drooped another fraction of an inch. "True," he said. "But you get the books."

"I'd like to be there when they arrive."

"I'll see if I can work it out. There's one more thing," he said, leaning back in his chair.

"What's that?"

"*Black Sun* is the only book of Abbey's I don't have in a signed edition."

"Actually, the date on that inscription is wrong."

"To me it doesn't matter. I'll be helping you and the library out and, uh, well, I . . ."

"You want me to give you *Black Sun*?" It was a book she hated to part with; it brought back memories of her last conversation with Burke. As one of the signed books in the collection, it also had evidentiary value.

"I am sticking my neck out for this place."

"I'll have to discuss it with Harrison."

"Claire, this seller has hot property. He—or she—is not going to wait around for long. There's nothing to stop the seller from offering the books to another dealer."

"I'll call you Monday."

"You do that," Rex said, standing up and putting his hat on his head.

Claire walked him to the side door. The minute he was outside,

131

he flicked his lighter and ignited the cigarette that was now dangling from his lip. "Are you driving back to Socorro tonight?" Claire asked.

"Not till morning," Rex said.

Claire supposed that meant that somewhere in Albuquerque a woman was waiting, maybe even the woman she'd seen him talking to. She watched him walk across the plaza, thinking that Rex had the longest legs she'd ever seen, the legs of a spider. The shadow walking beside him made them appear even longer.

The party was breaking up, and from where she stood, she could see the guests leaving. Gail walked across the plaza and entered the shadows under the balcony of the humanities building, where she was approached by another woman. Actually, Claire thought, accosted might be a better word. The other woman was wearing a black baseball cap, which would have hidden her face even if she weren't standing in the shadows. She gestured angrily at Gail, who started to walk away. The other woman followed, grabbed Gail's arm, and restrained her. At this point they stood beside the stairs leading to the balcony that circled the humanities building. They were arguing, but Claire couldn't hear anything from where she stood.

Mingling with some people who were leaving the party, she crossed the plaza and entered the humanities building from the far side. She climbed a flight of stairs and let herself onto the balcony, staying close to the shadows cast by the building. When she reached the corner, she peered around it quickly, then dropped below the wall, which was about three feet high. She caught a quick glimpse of Gail and the other woman standing nose to nose. From here she could hear clearly what they were saying.

"I told you I need the money," the other woman said. "I've already put my ass on the line for you more than once."

"I don't have it," Gail whined.

"Then, get it. I can give you a week. That's it. Meet me at the same place. Same time."

"Shit," Gail said.

She stomped back across the plaza while the woman headed in

the direction of Central. Claire stepped into the shadows of the humanities building and watched, noticing that Gail's adversary wore the black pants and basketball sneakers of a student. A gust of wind caught the black hat and lifted it from the woman's head. She reached up to catch it, but before she did, Claire caught a glimpse of a scalp that was bald as a man's.

CHAPTER ELEVEN

Over the weekend Claire tried Anthony again, but all she got for her trouble was Willie Nelson. Anthony could be anywhere in the Southwest, scouting or peddling his books. He might show up tomorrow. He might show up next year. He might never show up at all. Anthony was a free spirit.

On the other hand, she considered Rex to be a stingy spirit. He wasn't bad-looking and had once written a decent book. Still Claire couldn't figure out why women were so attracted to him. Rex was about as warm as the blue ice pack she kept in her freezer for camping trips, and he was obviously trouble. On Sunday he called to tell her he'd had further contact with his seller, and the seller had accepted his offer of twelve thousand dollars. "Have you discussed the deal with Harrison?" he asked.

Claire hadn't, but she'd had a day to think it over and had decided to go ahead. It was her money. It was her decision to make, not Harrison's. "I'll do it," she said.

"I'll need a cashier's check made out to cash."

"That's as good as handing you twelve thousand in bills," Claire replied.

"You've known me for ten years, Claire. Have I ever gone back on my word?"

"Not when it comes to books."

"You'll get your books. I guarantee it. And I won't accept them unless they are in perfect condition."

Claire took Rex at his word. He never had made much money writing, and since he'd stopped, selling books had become his only source of income. In this business, livelihood depended on reputation. If he deceived her, word would get out very quickly, and no one else in the book world would want to deal with Rex Barker. One hundred twelve thousand dollars might be enough for him to risk his way of life. Twelve thousand wasn't. Claire didn't quite trust Rex enough, however, to believe his story about the e-mail seller. Rex might already have the books in his possession, might have been the one who offered them to Page One, Too, might even have been the one who stole them from her truck. He might have already sold the Adams prints on the art market and discarded *The History of the Blue* as worthless.

"Did you ask about *Black Sun*?"

"I can't give you that book, Rex. Because of the inscription, the police will want it as evidence. I have a signed copy of my own I could give you."

There was a long pause, followed by a rather loud sigh, then Rex said, "All right. Can you bring the check down here tomorrow? I want to be ready whenever the books arrive." Socorro was eighty miles away, a town a person could live in dirt cheap. It was close enough to find women in Albuquerque if Rex wanted them, far enough away to discourage them from moving in.

"It's a long drive," Claire said. "Could you meet me halfway?"

There was a pause while Rex dodged the red flags that went up whenever he received a request from a woman. "How about the Walking Sands Rest Area?" he asked.

It was a sixty-mile drive for Claire, twenty for Rex, not halfway but a fair exchange in his mind. "All right," Claire agreed. "Monday at six?"

"I'll be there," Rex said.

On Monday morning Claire called Rachel to her office to discuss recent events. It had rained early in the day, leaving enough moisture in the air to turn Rachel's hair into ringlets that made her look even younger. "Could this Rex guy be our thief?" she asked Claire.

"It's possible. He comes up to Albuquerque a lot. He might have been at the university for some reason and seen the books in my truck. I'm sure he could use the money, but I don't know that he'd want it bad enough to ruin his reputation."

"It won't ruin his reputation unless he gets caught. I could try to set up another sting."

"How? According to Rex, the seller won't say when the books will be shipped or who will be shipping them. Do you have the time to sit around his house for days waiting for the books to show up?"

"No. I can't operate outside of Albuquerque, either, and I wouldn't expect much help from the local police. How do you feel about Rex? Do you trust him?"

"Far enough to produce the books."

"Will you see him again after this?"

"Our paths will cross; we're in the same business."

"If he's driving a new truck, then we'll know he's our man. Everyone in your business is always on the verge of vehicular meltdown."

"True," Claire said. Sometimes it seemed that all any bookseller wanted out of life was to keep a vehicle running. Their vehicles tended to be vans and trucks that could be used to transport books. Claire had seen a Chevy commercial playing over a background of zydeco music that summed up the attitude of booksellers she knew: "Wives leave you, friends forget you, bosses fire you; trucks are forever." Those booksellers lived on the brink of financial ruin, and when a vehicle died, it sent them over the brink. Why? Because they loved books or because they loved freedom? Claire wondered sometimes whether her financial security had kept her from fully experiencing life. She didn't think Rex enjoyed life any more than she did, but Anthony Barbour and John Harlan might.

"Insist on getting a receipt from the shipper. We may be able to track the seller that way."

"All right." Claire moved on to the next problem. "As I was leaving the Eliot Porter exhibit Friday night, I saw Gail standing beside the stairway to the Humanities Building arguing with another woman. I went upstairs and eavesdropped on them from the balcony. The other woman demanded that Gail pay her money."

"Did you get a good look at the other woman?"

"Not really. She was wearing a baseball cap and basketball sneakers. She took off her hat, and I could see that her head was totally bald. She was the same height as Gail."

"Could be a student."

"Or someone pretending to be a student. They made an appointment to meet again in a week."

"Did they say where or when?"

" 'Same time, same place,' the woman said."

"We'll keep an eye on the places the drug deals go down."

"Gail was in a car accident not long ago. I've seen her popping pills in the kitchen. She might have gotten addicted to a prescription painkiller."

"Let's hope she's not selling your books to support her habit. I've always suspected it was an inside job."

"I'm aware of that."

"Anything else?" Rachel got out of her chair, standing straight as a soldier. Claire was struck by the contrast between her exuberant hair and her military manner, but felt relieved all over again that she had found someone with enthusiasm for her job.

"That's it," Claire said.

She had already put the cashier's check she purchased for John Harlan back into her bank account. On her lunch hour she went to Norwest to get another. After work she drove to the Walking Sands Rest Area on I-25. There wasn't much to see on the interstate south of Albuquerque except for faraway mountains loping to Texas. This could be a drab gray moonscape, but when the sun set, the eastern mountains turned radiant in the afterglow and the western peaks were silhouetted against the fading light. A couple of dark clouds hovered over the Magdalenas, their sinuous shapes following the curves of the peaks. Lightning flashed from one cloud to another. Behind them the sky turned the color of a brilliant peach.

Claire wondered if the dark clouds and lightning were an omen. It seemed vaguely illicit to be meeting a man at a rest area and handing over twelve thousand dollars even if the man was Rex Barker and all she was getting for her money was rare books. Since the books were stolen property, she was supporting (possibly even encouraging) crime. Was she so different from the students who bought and sold drugs? Like other criminal acts, this one was fueled by a need bordering on an obsession: the criminal's need for money, her need to have the books back. She ought to be repelled by what she was doing, but she wasn't; she was excited.

Claire pulled off at Walking Sands just as the sun dropped behind the Magdalenas. Most of the rest areas in New Mexico had the rounded adobe shape of indigenous architecture, but this one looked like it belonged at the beach. It was a series of picnic areas tucked into wooden boxes and connected by boardwalks supported by posts stuck in the sandy soil. The sand around the buildings had been raked into the fine lines of a Japanese garden. A set of footprints crisscrossed the lines and lost definition in the sand. The rest area got its name from the way the sand shifted and blew. Rex's Silverado was alone in the parking lot. Claire got out of her truck and climbed the ramp to the boardwalk where Rex leaned against a post smoking. His long legs angled out like buttresses supporting the post. He wore a black leather jacket, jeans, and motorcycle boots.

"Did you bring it?" he asked.

"Yes." They were all alone in a clandestine setting full of electricity, but Claire felt no electrical charge whatsoever between her and Rex. She handed over the cashier's check. "The university police said to insist on a receipt from the shipper."

"No problem," replied Rex. He dropped his cigarette to the boardwalk and ground it out with the heel of his boot. "I'm coming up to 'burque over the weekend. If I get the books in time, I'll bring 'em back to you then."

"Thanks," Claire said.

They walked down the ramp with Rex's heels tapping a staccato beat and lightning flashing over the Magdalenas. They got in their vehicles, and Claire headed north to Albuquerque while Rex went back to Socorro.

She spent an anxious week dodging Harrison and getting very little sleep. On Friday afternoon Rex showed up in her office with the books. They had been shipped UPS in the very same box in which they had been stolen, with Claire's writing on the top stating they were valuable. The missing history and folio left some space in the box, which had been filled with bubble wrap.

"I looked at them and checked the inscriptions before I handed over the money," Rex said. "They're very fine."

He knew Claire wouldn't accept his word for it and waited while she examined each book. "You're right," she said. "They look as if they haven't even been touched."

"Did you bring *Black Sun*?"

Claire handed it over.

"Anything else?"

"The receipt?"

Rex handed over the slip from UPS. The sender's name and address had been filled in as William Bonney, Lincoln, New Mexico, although the books had been mailed from Albuquerque. "The thief has a sense of humor," Rex said.

"Wouldn't you think someone at UPS would notice that the shipper was William Bonney aka Billy the Kid?"

"Not really," Rex said. His hand reached for a cigarette, indicating it was time to leave. "Is that it?"

"Where did you park? In the lot by the bookstore?"

"Yeah."

"I have to go to the bookstore. I'll walk you to your car."

Rex said little as they walked across the campus. Claire bid him good-bye at the parking lot's tollbooth, but lingered until she saw him open the door of his old Silverado.

Rachel took the receipt to UPS, but all they could tell her was that the books had been shipped COD uninsured from Albuquerque by someone who claimed to be William Bonney and asked for a cashier's check made out to cash. Claire made a copy of the receipt and took it to the insurance company, along with the police report. The books had been appraised, the theft had been reported, Claire anticipated she would be reimbursed but expected it to take forever. Harrison issued a memo saying he "took enormous pride and delight in the return of the books to their rightful place, where they would be safeguarded in the appropriate manner." That meant he displayed the books on a shelf near his interior window so everybody walking by could see them. Whenever Claire did pass by, her joy in seeing the books was diminished by her annoyance at Harrison's arrogance.

She called John Harlan to tell him she'd gotten the books back.

"*Muy bueno,*" he said. "I'm happy for you."

"I only wish I'd gotten them all back."

"The Adams prints will turn up on the art market in New York or Santa Fe. You might as well forget about the history. I'll be out of town for a few days, but would you like to go to dinner next weekend to celebrate?"

"I can't," Claire replied. "I'm going back to the Blue."

Before she went home that night, she walked through the Eliot Porter exhibit thinking that Porter, like Mozart, sought harmony. Order had been restored in this corner of Claire's world, but there remained the issue of Burke's will.

CHAPTER TWELVE

When Claire called the ranch to say she was coming, Corinne answered the phone.

"How are you doing, Corinne?" Claire asked.

"All right," she replied, but her voice had the sound of an empty house with wind blowing in through broken windows.

"Will Jed be around? I'd like to talk to him while I'm there."

"He's gone to work for the Stoners," Corinne said. "Do you want their number?"

"Please."

Claire called the Stoners and got an answering machine saying no one was available at the Black Diamond Ranch. She left a message saying she'd be there on Friday to talk to Jed.

Spring comes early in New Mexico, and Claire saw the first signs of it as she drove to the Blue. It was late February, which in Albuquerque meant green shoots of crocuses and budding elm trees. But on the highway spring meant wind, wind that threatened to pick her up and deposit her in the fast lane, wind that turned her truck into a bucking bronco, forcing her to hold tight to the steering wheel. Winter was mild at the I-40 latitude; but spring could be a cruel season. That was when New Mexico became known as the place Arizona blew through on its way to Texas.

Since Sheriff Henner could be out anywhere on the thousands of miles of highways he patrolled, Claire had made an appointment to see him. She arrived in Reserve right on time at 2:30. In the half a minute it took to walk from her truck to his office, the wind whipped her hair into a frenzy.

"Pleasure to see you, Ms. Reynier," the sheriff said, smiling with his eyes while his face fell into reptilian wrinkles. Claire smoothed her hair into place. "Windy out there."

"It is," she replied.

"Long drive?"

"Four hours."

"Can I get you a cup of coffee?"

"No thanks."

"Mind if I have one?"

"Go ahead."

The sheriff filled a mug from a pot that seemed to be perpetually brewing and led Claire into his office, where he sat down and motioned her to do the same. He leaned back in his chair. "I suppose you want to know how the investigation is going."

"That's why I am here."

"Well, we got the report back from the OMI. The drug screen showed alcohol and a benzodiazepine in Burke's bloodstream, but not enough to kill him."

"Enough to impair his judgment?"

Henner took a sip of his coffee. "Now, that would be a hard thing to establish, wouldn't it? It might depend on how much judgment a person had to begin with. I saw Burke not long before he died, and in my opinion his judgment was fine. I'd say he knew what he was doing, but you could find a lawyer who'd take a look at the same facts and interpret them differently."

"What was the cause of death?"

"Exposure. So the DA had to consider what caused Burke to die of exposure. It happens often enough in Catron County that a man chooses to die when he sees his health and his power slipping away, but when a man gets to that point, usually he puts a bullet through his head. It's messy, but it's quick."

142

He looked at Claire as if he was expecting a reaction, but she kept her expression purposely blank.

"When someone freezes to death, it's an Indian who's drunk and twenty miles from nowhere. In all my years in law enforcement, I have never seen anyone deliberately die that way, but the Eskimos do it, so I guess it can't be too bad. Sooner or later, I hear, you just go to sleep. The DA had to decide whether his death was Burke's choice or Mariah's. The family was madder than a nest of hornets, but that didn't help them any because the DA can get ornery if he thinks someone is telling him how to do his job. The question was if Burke didn't want to go, how did Mariah get him out under that tree? There was nothing to indicate a struggle—no bruises, no torn clothes. Mariah's strong, Burke was weak, but was she strong enough to carry him or drag him? There is nothing to indicate that she did. He wasn't injected with drugs. He was perfectly capable of taking the Valium on his own. The DA concluded that there wasn't sufficient evidence to prosecute Mariah Geraty for murder or assisted suicide, and get a conviction here. Now, whether what she did was right or not, everybody'll have to make their own decision." It was a long speech for Henner, and he leaned back in his chair and took a deep breath. "You comfortable with that?"

"No, but more comfortable than I would be with a prosecution."

"Burke gave you a tough job."

"True."

"He must have felt you were up to it."

"I hope so," Claire replied. "I need to look up something at the county clerk's office. Can you tell me where it is?"

"Right around the corner," Sheriff Henner said.

"Thanks for your help."

"Glad to do it." He put down his mug and walked her to the door.

Claire found the office in the basement of the courthouse. The clerk, Janet Randall, dressed like the coal miner's daughter. Her dyed brown hair tumbled in curls to her shoulders. Her white blouse was trimmed with eyelet, and her denim skirt had broomstick pleats. Her silver concho belt looked as if it weighed five pounds. Her cowboy boots had pointed toes and high heels. Claire was startled to find someone so decked out in Catron County, home of the casual cowboy.

"No problem," Janet said when Claire told her who she was and that she wanted to see the deed to the Lovell ranch. She flounced her skirt as she stepped into the back room, but came back shortly with the deed.

"That was quick," Claire said.

"Honey, I've been doin' this for thirty years. I know where every deed is recorded and every skeleton lies buried in Catron County."

And did her job well enough to dress as she pleased. It took courage for a working woman to wear ruffles in the 1990s. Claire inspected the deed and everything seemed to be in order. She could attach no significance to the fact that the original had not been in Burke's desk. The ranch was transferred from Benjamin deWitt to Burke P. Lovell in 1972. There were a number of liens on the property that were paid off in the year before the transfer. Claire totaled them in her head, and came up with over one hundred thousand dollars. "Benjamin deWitt owed a lot of money," she said.

"He was a gambler," Janet replied. "When he got sick, Burke paid off the debts so Ben could live out his last year in peace. In return, Ben left him the ranch." She looked up through lashes that were thick with mascara. "And now it will be going to someone else?"

Claire suspected that a woman who knew where all the skeletons were buried in Catron County also knew who was getting the ranch. "Burke left the property to Mariah Geraty," she said.

"Ah," replied Janet.

"Can you make me a copy of this?" She handed over the deed.

"Sure."

"I understand that Benjamin deWitt wrote a history of the Blue," Claire said when Janet came back with the copy.

"He did."

"I'm a librarian at UNM. I'm interested in regional histories, but I haven't been able to find deWitt's book anywhere."

"I don't think it was a best-seller," Janet laughed. "Ben was no

Danielle Steele. Did you try the local library? Right around the corner?"

"No, but I will."

"If you can't find it there, you could try askin' Ben's sisters. He had two. One of 'em, Ellen, died recently in Globe, Arizona, but the other one—her name is Bobbye Johnson—lives in Datil." Janet wrote down Bobbye's phone number and directions to her house for Claire. "She'd be pleased to know the university is interested in Ben's book."

Claire suspected that as soon as she walked out the door, Janet would be on the phone, and by the time she left Reserve, everyone in town would know she'd been there and why. It was unnerving to think that a visit from her could qualify as an event. It might be pleasant to live in town where so much—the library, the post office, the courthouse, the sheriff—was within walking distance. The down side was that everybody in town knew your business. As Claire rounded the corner she turned into the wind that came blasting out of Arizona. She put her head down, turned up her collar, and wondered whether she would find *The History of the Blue* in the Reserve Library. It was the most logical place for it to be, but its absence from the other libraries was not a good omen. Claire's reason told her she might well find one, but her intuition intimated she would not. She asked herself why she was even looking now that the library had all the novels back. Why not accept John's conclusion that the thief had discarded the history as worthless?

If the history did start showing up, it would support Rachel's theory that Gail or Rex had stolen the box of books and John's theory that the history had been discarded. Rachel had made it clear that she suspected Gail first and Rex second in the theft. She was probably right, Claire thought. They fit the profile, they were the logical suspects, but neither of them satisfied her; Gail was too obvious, Rex too predictable, and both were too close to home. If she continued to find holes on the shelves where the history had been, it would open the field and suggest there was a thief out there with an unknown motive. Rachel was likely to consider expanding the investigation a waste of time and money, but the possibility appealed to Claire.

She entered the library wrapped in a mixture of anticipation and dread, logged onto the computer, hit the A button for author, and typed in the name of Benjamin deWitt. *The History of the Blue* came up. Claire copied down the call number and went hunting in the shelves. Once again, she found an empty space where the history should have been. She approached a young man with sandy hair who sat at the reference desk reading.

"Excuse me," she said. "I'm looking for a history of the Blue that was written by Benjamin deWitt."

"Did you check the computer?"

"Yes. It's not where it should be shelved."

"Who knows? Could be anywhere." He shrugged and went back to his book.

As she inched her truck down the *caracol* that led into the Blue, Claire felt the wind diminish. It seemed to follow a trajectory that took it across the flats and smashed it into the mountains without dipping into the valley. The sense of being sheltered and protected was part of the charm of the Blue. The ranch still looked like a remote and calm paradise. Burr grazed in his corral. Smoke rose from the chimney. Claire was greeted at the door by Roamer and Corinne, who wore a baggy cardigan sweater with the sleeves pulled down to her wrists. Mariah and Eric were waiting in the hallway. Eric said hello, and Mariah gave her a hug.

Claire settled into the guest bedroom, and a half hour later they sat down to dinner. She was introduced to the new ranch hand, Pete, who was in his mid-twenties, had lots of curly hair, and dressed like an environmentalist or a lumberjack in a plaid shirt, jeans, and thick-soled hiking boots. He was around 5′10″ and had the arms and shoulders of a weight lifter. If Pete was Mariah's boyfriend, Claire thought, she'd met her match. Pete complimented Corinne on the roast, filled his plate three times, and had two helpings of cherry pie.

He and Orin Stoner were about the same age, and were living

only a few miles apart. A visitor from another culture—or another planet—might see little difference between them. They both wore jeans, boots, and long-sleeved shirts, but Orin's clothes were new and immaculate. Pete's were old and messy. Old and messy indicated to Claire that the wearer came from a background of privilege. New and neat said the wearer was hoping to achieve a life of privilege. Liberal for the first, conservative for the second. Environmentalist. Rancher. A few miles distant. Poles apart.

To test her supposition Claire questioned Pete across the dining room table. "Did you know Mariah before you took this job?" she asked.

"We met when I was living in Phoenix," Mariah answered.

"I was ready to get out of the city. She offered me this job; I took it," Pete said.

"What were you doing in Phoenix?" Claire asked.

"I was a zookeeper in charge of the Mexican wolf exhibit. I met Mariah when she brought Eric to see the wolves."

"Wolf is a four-letter word in the Blue," Claire said.

Pete shrugged. "I'm not intimidated. Whether the ranchers like it or not, the wolves will be reintroduced."

He had something else in common with Mariah, Claire thought, a kind of boldness that verged on bravado.

"I teach Eric that wolves have as much right to be here as ranchers," Mariah said.

Mariah was right in theory, Claire knew, but she was anxious about how those beliefs would play out in practice.

The meal was like every other Claire had eaten here. The food was delicious but the conversation was strained, and she couldn't wait for dinner to be over. As soon as she finished her pie, she excused herself and walked through the dark house to Burke's office. The living room and the den separated the office from the rest of the house. Mariah had gone outside with Pete and Eric to look at an alignment of the planets. Corinne was straightening up the kitchen, but even the churning sound of the dishwasher couldn't be heard from Burke's office. Claire thought that living in a house in which there was room to disappear could make it easier to get along with incompatible people. The silence in the office was intense. "Didn't you foresee all this squabbling?" she asked Burke's memory. "Did you really want Mariah to have the ranch at the expense of your other children?" He didn't answer, so she turned on the computer and listened to it hum. The Windows icons dotted the screen. Claire studied them, wondering if the e-mail that came from anon.net.fi could have emanated from here. She found no sign of an Internet server, and she couldn't remember ever receiving an e-mail from Burke. Maybe he hadn't used the Internet, or maybe he had and the account had been canceled. Claire had found no record of it when she went through his bills. She turned off the computer and faced the ancient Corona typewriter sitting on the desk. The Corona company had recently gone out of business because there was no more demand for typewriters. What had once been the name of a state-of-the-art machine was now the name of a beer. Had Burke kept the Corona for addressing envelopes and filling out forms or because it was an antique? If so, was it his antique or Ben's? How much of the stuff in this house had Benjamin deWitt left behind?

Claire slid a piece of paper into the platen and typed out Burke P. Lovell's name. It didn't appear to be the same type that she'd seen on the birth certificate, but she took the piece of paper with her to compare when she got back home. She decided to go to bed. As she walked through the dark and silent house, she thought about Benjamin deWitt. Had he lived in this huge house all by himself? she wondered. Where had he written his elusive book? Why was that book never where it ought to be?

Claire went to sleep in the downstairs bedroom and dreamed she was in a library with walls that were two stories high and full of books. The only way to access the books on the upper level was by a ladder on wheels. She was standing on it, reaching for something, when the wheels began to roll and the books to tumble off the shelves. Books fell all around her and crashed to the floor. The ladder wobbled, and Claire fell, too, landing on the pile of books. The books should have felt like hard, angular elbows, but she woke with a pillow under her. It was early morning. Light came in through the window and swept away the darkness. Claire had to go to the bathroom, but she waited until she smelled coffee brewing and heard sounds in the kitchen before she got up.

When she entered the kitchen, she found Corinne sitting at the table eating cereal with the sleeves of her bathrobe pulled down to her wrists. Claire poured herself a coffee and sat down beside her.

"I met Janet Randall yesterday," she began.

"How is Janet?" Corinne asked. "I haven't seen her for ages."

"She seems fine. Has she had that job for long?"

"Forever," Corinne said. "She's older than she looks."

"She told me she knows where all the skeletons in Catron County are buried."

"She probably does."

"She gave me a copy of the deed to the ranch. There were a number of liens on the property that your father paid off. Ben owed a lot of money."

"He was a gambler," Corinne said.

"Did he live in this big house all by himself?"

"Ben usually had a woman around. Sometimes Dad came over from Tucson on weekends."

Pete opened the porch door and let himself in, along with a blast of cold air. He wore a down vest over his plaid shirt. Pete was a good-looking guy, and Claire couldn't help wondering if he had spent the night in the hired hand's trailer or upstairs with Mariah. "Mornin'," he said, helping himself to a cup of coffee.

"Morning," Claire replied.

"Sometimes this kitchen has a real bad smell, Corinne, like an animal crawled under the floorboards and died. I notice it more when I've come in from outside," Pete said.

Corinne ate her cereal and didn't reply. Claire didn't smell anything, but she'd woken up feeling congested from all the wood smoke in the valley.

Mariah and Eric came down, and Corinne cooked breakfast. When the meal was over, Claire told Mariah she wanted to talk to her. Pete took Eric out to the barn, Corinne cleaned up, and Claire and Mariah put on their jackets and went out to the porch, where they sat down in the rocking chairs. A couple of ravens flew across the field and settled into the bare branches of a cottonwood, looking like punctuation marks in the sky.

"I talked to Sheriff Henner yesterday," Claire began. "He told me that the DA has decided not to prosecute."

"I know," said Mariah.

"That must be a relief."

"It is." Mariah smiled. She had perfect white teeth and a beautiful complexion with cheeks that turned to roses when touched by the cold. Her black hair was thick and tousled. Claire thought that every mournful Irish ballad she had ever heard might have been written about Mariah. The women in the songs had the same pale skin and dark power. Young and fresh as she was, Mariah had participated in the awful finality of death and, once she had done that, what else might she be capable of? Mariah had crossed a barrier and entered the place where veterans and criminals go, a place Claire could only contemplate. She knew very little about Mariah's background and whether there was something in her past that had conditioned her to participate in Burke's death. Or had her involvement been circumstantial? Would Claire have assisted Burke if he had asked for her help? She didn't think so. A raven squawked, breaking her concentration and bringing her back to this moment when Mariah sat rocking in the adjacent chair.

"The news isn't all good," Claire said.

"Oh?"

"My lawyer and I had a meeting with Samantha, James, and their lawyer. They intend to contest the terms of the will."

"On what grounds?" Mariah put her foot down to stop the forward motion of her chair.

It was the moment Claire had been dreading. "That Burke was incapacitated and a victim of undue influence when he signed the will. That you deceived him. That you are not his daughter."

Mariah jumped out of her chair and stood with her arms crossed, rubbing her hands against the sleeves of her jacket. "That's a lie," she cried.

"My lawyer suggested I hire a genealogical search company to see if there were any other heirs. They found your birth certificate on record, and it did not list Burke as your father."

"Who did it list?"

"No one. That line was empty."

"Then, how do *you* think Burke's name got on there?"

"I don't know."

"I didn't add it," Mariah said. She let go of her arms, dropped her hands to her sides, and clenched her hands into fists. "When I first saw the birth certificate, it had Burke's name on it."

"Could it have been your mother?"

"I don't know. I showed it to Burke, and he didn't question it. Isn't that what matters?"

"The family's lawyer is very aggressive, Mariah. You need to get one, too, to protect your interests."

"A lawyer?" Mariah responded, as if Claire had suggested she get in bed with a snake.

"You could prove you are Burke's daughter by taking a DNA test."

"Burke was cremated," Mariah said. "What would you test DNA with?"

"There must be hair or something left here that a sample could be taken from. It doesn't take very much. If you're related by blood to the other family members, comparison to their DNA would establish that."

Mariah put her hands in her pockets and planted her feet on the floor. "Why should *I* have to take a DNA test?" she demanded. "No one's asking Samantha or James or Corinne to submit to DNA testing, are they?"

"Burke has always acknowledged them as his children. He raised them."

"Well, he didn't do a very good job of it, did he?"

"Corinne didn't come to the meeting. How does she feel about the lawsuit? Do you know?"

"We haven't discussed it."

"Would you consider settling? Burke thought you could use the money he left you for that purpose if need be."

"They won't be content with two hundred thousand. They want the ranch." Claire saw Pete walking across the yard with Eric balanced on his shoulders. The three of them could constitute a family, she thought, and turn this into a happy place. Mariah and Pete had the strength and the determination. They reminded Claire of settlers—proud of their ability to conquer obstacles, so proud they might go out of their way to create them. She excused herself and went into the house.

Claire's head had cleared while she was outside. The instant she stepped into the kitchen, she smelled the rotting animal smell. She remembered what the psychologist had said about a cutter's wounds festering, and she feared the smell might be coming from under the long sleeves of Corinne, who was unloading the dishwasher.

"Did you ever consider moving into Reserve, Corinne?" she asked. "It seems to have a nice, supportive community. You might be happier with more people around."

Corinne gave her a look of such desperation that Claire felt it entering into her pores and despaired that whatever she tried to do to help would be a mistake. Corinne lived in a glass house, and Claire feared that calling attention to her disturbed behavior would shatter the glass.

She went into the office and called the Black Diamond Ranch. Karen Stoner answered the phone.

"We got your message," she said. "Are you coming over?"

"I'd like to. What time would be good for you?"

"How about right now?"

"I'll be there," Claire said.

CHAPTER THIRTEEN

As the raven flew the Black Diamond was only a few miles away. To drive there Claire had to cross the river, follow the dirt road for three miles, and turn down the next driveway, which ended at the Stoners' house, a single-story stucco far more modest than Burke's massive log cabin. A Ford truck was parked in front of the house. A satellite dish gathered information in the yard. A golden retriever barked and ran out to greet her. Orin Stoner opened the front door with Karen standing beside him. Claire thought how close this couple was geographically to Mariah and Pete, but how far away in attitude. The valley would be a better place if they could learn to get along.

"Howdy," Orin Stoner said as Claire approached the door.

"Hello," she replied. "Is Jed here? I was hoping to talk to him."

"He had to go into town," Orin said.

"He said he was sorry to miss you," Karen added. "Why don't you come on in?"

Claire followed them inside, thinking that the Stoners seemed more concerned about their animals than they did about their house, which smelled like a kennel. The sofa and armchairs were furry with dog hair. The coffee table was a wagon wheel with a glass top. There were no pictures on the walls, but two rifles were mounted over the fireplace. The only reading material in sight was a newsletter from the Cattlegrowers Association. The Stoners, who both wore jeans and Western shirts, sank into the sofa. The golden retriever jumped up beside them and laid its head in Karen's lap. Claire lowered herself into a deep armchair. Orin focused his intense blue eyes on her, and she felt they were magnets holding her in place.

"What brings you over to the Blue?" he asked.

"I'm settling up Burke's estate."

"How's that going?" asked Karen.

Once again, Claire had the sensation that everybody in the Blue knew exactly what everybody else was doing and exactly how everything was going. "There have been some disagreements," she admitted.

"Is that why you wanted to talk to Jed?" Karen's eyes were more like butterflies than magnets, flitting from Claire to Orin and back again.

"It is," Claire said.

"He wanted to be here," Orin said. "He just had some business in town he had to take care of."

"When will he be back?"

"Not till Monday."

"Could I catch up to him in Reserve?"

"Could, but I don't know where he'll be. Have you ever seen a working ranch?" Orin asked. "It would be our pleasure to show you around."

"I'm afraid I don't have time," Claire said. "I need to get back to Albuquerque."

"It's a great way of life we have here."

"I'm sure it is."

"There are people out there who are trying to take it away from us. They want to bring the wolves back, and if they do, it'll be devastating to our cattle. That guy who's working at the Lovells now is an environmentalist and a wolf lover. He's talkin' Mariah into letting the federal government put holding pens for the wolves there. One of those wolves gets loose, hell, it'll be heading right for us."

Karen patted the golden retriever. "Our dogs won't be safe, our

154

cattle won't be safe, and when we have kids they won't be safe, either."

Claire was tired of listening to ranchers whine about the big, bad wolf. The area had plenty of predators—foxes, coyotes, black bear, bobcats, mountain lions. She didn't believe that wolf reintroduction would change the balance of power much; man would always be at the top of the food chain in the Blue. She glanced at the rifles that were suspended over the fireplace. They were the levelers that would keep man on top, bullets being far more effective than teeth and claws.

"If we owned the Lovell ranch, we'd get back the BLM leases Burke gave up and use the land for what it was intended for—grazing cattle," Karen added.

Claire thought that if the land was intended for anything, it would be predators not cattle—the predators had been there first—but that was an old issue and Karen had just raised a new one. "Even if Burke's ranch were to be sold," she said, "it's worth over two million dollars." The question that hung in the air was, how could a young couple like the Stoners afford it?

"A rancher's life is dangerous," Orin replied. "You're working with powerful machinery and animals all the time. There's always the possibility you're gonna get injured or killed. My daddy held a lot of insurance."

"He provided for us," Karen said.

"You're thinking of buying Burke's ranch?" Claire asked, trying to hide the dismay she felt.

"We got the down payment from the insurance. We talked to the bank, and they're willing to finance the rest."

"That's a little premature, isn't it? The will hasn't even been probated yet."

"Samantha and James said they'd sell to us if they get the property," Karen replied. "They won't want to be managing a ranch from Santa Fe and Phoenix. We don't need that big old house. We'd let Corinne go on living there as long as she wants to. She's not doin' too well since her daddy died. We'd check in on her. We'd look after her. Jed and Kass both agree that Burke didn't have his faculties when he signed that will."

"He sure as hell wouldn't have mentioned The Nature Conservancy if he did," added Orin.

Karen straightened the barrettes that held her hair in place. "You're the only one left who thinks he knew what he was doin'," she said to Claire.

"You've got credibility. If you were to testify that Burke was incompetent, you would sway any judge," Orin said.

"I won't do that," Claire replied.

Orin leaned against the back of the sofa, put his boots up on the wagon wheel table, and folded his arms across his chest. "Why not?"

Claire sat up even straighter in her chair. "I don't believe he *was* incompetent. I believe the will reflects Burke's wishes."

"You're sure about that?" Orin's eyes remained focused on Claire.

"Isn't the issue what Burke wanted? I believe he wanted Mariah to have the ranch and that he wanted it to be a nature preserve." Orin's cold blue eyes responded that the issue for him was what *he* wanted. Lean and hard as Orin was, he was a spoiled rancher's son accustomed to getting his way, and not intending to stop now. Claire felt chilled, as if a vulture had flown between her and the sun.

"I guess we got nothin' more to talk about." Orin unfolded his arms and put his feet on the floor.

"I guess not," Claire replied. The Stoners got off the sofa, and they walked down the hallway with the dog padding along behind them. As they passed the open door of the room the Stoners used for an office, Claire noticed that they had a PC and that it was turned on.

Driving up the winding dirt road that led out of the Blue, Claire understood that a process which began when Benjamin deWitt left his ranch to the outsider, Burke Lovell, would culminate if Mariah took title and allowed the federal government to use the property as a staging area for the reintroduction of the Mexican gray wolf. The Blue would change, whether people here liked it or not.

Claire passed the Silver Spur Saloon on her way through Reserve, a rambling barn of a place. It was four o'clock in the afternoon and already the parking lot was filling up. She could have used a drink after her visit to the Stoners, but she wasn't a woman to drink alone in a bar. Nevertheless, she pulled into the parking lot. It occurred to her that if Jed had gone into Reserve, he could be sitting on a bar stool or at least the bartender might know where he was.

Claire had never been a woman whose looks stopped conversation when she walked into a bar, so she was surprised by the ripple of silence that followed her entrance. She attributed it to being a stranger, and sat down on an empty stool, trying to blend into the crowd while Shania Twain sang and the conversation started up again.

"Help you?" the bartender asked. She was a middle-aged woman with cheeks that had weathered into corrugated cardboard, a determined jaw, and a mouth painted don't-mess-with-me red. She looked like she could handle herself in a roomful of cowboys.

"I'm looking for Jed Acker, who used to work for Burke Lovell." A quick glance around the room had assured Claire that Jed wasn't present.

"He's workin' for the Stoners now."

"So I hear."

"When he comes to town he stops in for a quick one, but I haven't seen him recently. Anybody here seen Jed?" she yelled.

No one had, or if they had, they weren't willing to admit it. "Get you a drink?"

"I'd like a real ginger ale if you have it." Ginger ale was Claire's favorite drink, and there weren't many places that served it anymore. Some restaurants made a manufactured version with Sprite and Coke, but she didn't consider that drinkable.

"Coming up," the bartender said.

When the drink arrived, Claire handed the bartender her business card. "If Jed shows up, would you tell him I'd like to talk to him?"

The frame of the mirror was stuffed full of business cards, and the bartender stuck Claire's into the crack between the mirror and the wood. "Sure," she said, moving on to the next customer, too busy to ask why Claire wanted to talk to Jed.

Claire drove as far as Datil that night, watching the horizon take on the blue-green glow of a Maxfield Parrish painting. What seemed surreal in a work of art became all too real out here. Venus appeared in the west followed one by one by the stars. Claire checked into a motel in Datil and in the morning went looking for Ben deWitt's sister, Bobbye Johnson. Datil was on the high Plains of San Agustín. Even for the west, the space was enormous—miles upon miles of tumbleweed, sage, and grazing cattle interrupted occasionally by a ranch house wrapped in a circle of wind-bent trees. Out here it was easy to feel like a particle of dust in an infinite universe. Claire enjoyed the experience of driving through the Plains of San Agustín, but she never wanted to linger; the space overwhelmed her.

The county clerk, Janet Randall, had given good directions, with none of the superfluous details that can be confusing. Claire turned down one dirt road, then another, and easily found the mailbox with the Johnson name on it and the white trailer that Bobbye called home. There were no other buildings in sight. A large Chevy sedan was parked in front of the trailer.

A dog began to bark the minute Claire closed the door of her truck. It had the high-strung yap of a small breed that compensates in noise and aggression for what it lacks in size. "Be quiet, Buddy," she heard a woman's voice yell from inside the trailer. The woman opened the door, enveloped in a cloud of smoke and holding a cigarette in one hand. The dog at her heels was a small yellow mutt that paid no attention to its mistress's commands. The woman was about five feet tall with gray hair chopped into a ragged page boy and a face weathered like old wood. Claire placed her in her mid-seventies, old for a smoker.

"I'm looking for Bobbye Johnson."

"You found her."

Claire introduced herself and handed Bobbye her card. "A librarian. I guess it will be safe to let you in," Bobbye chuckled.

Claire dreaded entering a trailer filled with smoke, but she followed Bobbye inside. The interior of the trailer was surprisingly spacious and neat. Lace curtains on the windows framed the vast view. There was plenty of shelf space for books, but Claire didn't see any. All she saw shelved here was a collection of salt and pepper shakers. An overflowing ashtray sat on a Formica-topped table. Bobbye emptied it into the trash before sitting down and motioning Claire to join her.

"What can I do for you?" she asked.

"I've been trying to find a copy of your brother's history of the Blue."

"Why?"

"There was a copy in the collection Burke Lovell left to the library. It got stolen from my truck along with some other books. I've been trying to replace it, but I can't find one anywhere."

"I gave mine to the library in Reserve years ago."

"I looked. It's not there," Claire said.

Bobbye took a kitchen match from a box that was on the table and lit another cigarette. The dog barked when she struck the match. "Quiet, Buddy," she said. "My sister, Ellen, held onto hers. I thought I'd find it in her things after she died, but I didn't."

"What happened to your sister?"

Bobbye exhaled. "She had a violent death. You could say she was murdered."

"Murdered? How?"

"Her house in Globe was gettin' robbed, and she walked in on the robbers. They shot her three times with a thirty-eight. Wanted to make sure she was good and dead, I guess. My sister was a gentle person. She wouldn'ta hurt a soul. I keep a gun in my purse and another one under my pillow. Anybody who tries to harm me won't live long enough to regret it, but Ellen, she never kept a weapon. She trusted people. That was her mistake."

"When did the robbery happen?"

"About a month ago."

"Were the robbers caught?"

"No."

"How do you know there was more than one?"

"The police in Globe decided that on account of the prints they left and the trouble they caused. The house was a wreck. Her books and clothes were emptied all over the floor. You would have thought they were lookin' for drugs, exceptin' that Ellen was too old for the kind of drugs they wanted. All Ellen had was hormones and her blood pressure medicine."

"What did they take?" Claire asked.

"A TV, a VCR, costume jewelry, cash. The usual stuff. Ellen didn't have anything very valuable. It did seem strange that her copy of Ben's book was missing. My sister loved books. It wouldn't have been like her to get rid of it. But she mighta leant it to somebody and forgot to get it back. I didn't think too much about it, to tell you the truth, until you showed up. You think it was stolen from her house?"

"It's possible."

"Why would anybody steal Ben's book?"

Claire remembered the copies of *The Banditti of the Plains* that were either bought up or stolen by the cattlemen in Wyoming. "There may be some information in it someone wants to suppress."

Bobbye was skeptical. "What could that be? Burke brought me a copy when it came out. I never actually read it, but as far as I know, all it said was who settled where when and who married who. Ben read all the time, so he thought he could be a writer, but he drank too much. All he had in him was that one book. Killed himself with all his drinking. I thought he might have found happiness and love near the end, but it didn't work out. Nothin' in Ben's life ever worked out. As soon as it seemed like it was going to, he'd wreck it. Our mother loved that boy too much. He was her only son and all he ever did was disappoint."

"He did have that beautiful property that he passed on to Burke."

"Oh, it's beautiful, all right, but it always was an unhappy place. It's where I was raised, but I'd never want to live there again; there's too much contention in the Blue. Disagree with anybody down there, and you'll get shot for your trouble. It didn't bother me none that the ranch went to Burke. He deserved it; he was always bailing Ben out. I hated the way Ben lived—the gambling, the drinking, the women. By the time he died, we were barely speaking, so he had no reason to leave the place to me. I'd rather be up here in my trailer than down there in that huge house anyway. Here I've got space and sunshine all around me." She looked out the window at the distant blue mountains and the view that went on forever. "I don't like ownin' anything I've got to protect. It's too damn much trouble. I don't even lock my doors. I keep a gun to protect Buddy and me, but if anybody wants my stuff they're welcome to it."

"Has anyone ever tried to rob you?"

"Naah. There's nothing to steal. You know, though, I did come home once right after Ellen died feeling things weren't right. Nothing was missing, and I figured I was just made nervous by what happened to Ellen. You think I should be worried?" She put another cigarette in her mouth and let it dangle from her lip while she pulled a match from the box. Buddy sat up to watch and his claws scraped the floor.

Claire stared out the window at the faraway mountains. There was plenty to worry about if someone was willing to kill in order to obtain a copy of Benjamin deWitt's *History of the Blue.* Too many coincidences had become, in her mind, an enemy action. But the thieves resembled the clouds that cast their shadows on the distant mountains and moved on. She suspected they'd already been here, hadn't found what they wanted, and gone elsewhere. But where? Did they know about Anthony Barbour? It hadn't been hard for her to discover he had a copy. "I suspect they've gone elsewhere, but it might be wise to start locking your door," she said.

Bobbye struck her match, and Buddy barked on cue. "What difference would it make out here? Someone could load the trailer on a flatbed and move it down the road before anybody would notice."

"At least when you came home, you'd know whether anybody had been inside. You'd be less likely to walk in on a robbery in progress."

"You know what? If it comes right down to it, I'd rather die that way . . ." She cocked her fingers into the shape of a revolver and sited down the barrel. "Than this." She lifted her cigarette and watched the rising smoke.

CHAPTER FOURTEEN

On the drive back to Albuquerque, Claire thought about all she'd discovered on her trip. She intended to pass the information on to Rachel as soon as she reached the office on Monday, but she was left with the rest of Sunday to think about it. When she got home, Nemesis greeted her at the door, rubbed against her legs, and meowed to go out.

"In a minute," Claire said.

She understood the feeling Bobbye Johnson had when she came home and sensed things weren't right. Claire had once heard it described as the sensation that everything in your house has been removed and replaced by its exact replica. She didn't think it was possible to get into her house without jimmying a lock or breaking a window. Before she opened the door, she circled the house and saw no sign of forced entry. Nevertheless, once she was inside, Claire examined all the rooms, searching for anything out of order.

"Has anybody been in here?" she asked Nemesis. Even if he could speak, would he know or care? Nemesis was not a guard cat. All that mattered to him was getting fed and petted—going in, going out.

Everything was in place. Even the air seemed undisturbed. If people were robbing and killing for *The History of the Blue,* it made no sense to break into this house, since Claire's copy had already been stolen. Still knowing there was someone capable of such acts made her nervous. She thought about calling John Harlan and asking him to meet her somewhere for dinner. His clearheaded cynicism could drive out the cobwebs of suspicion. If she went out, however, she'd have to come home again after dark.

She checked the call screening box. Several calls from Unavailable, one from Madelyn. The light blinked once on the answering machine. Claire pushed the button and heard Madelyn say, "Just checking to see how you were."

She called Madelyn back and left a message on her machine saying she was fine, then she logged onto the computer and found the usual collection of e-mail flotsam: easy money, sleazy sex. No messages about books. She logged off the computer and called Anthony Barbour to find him on the road again.

"It's Claire, Anthony," she said to his machine. "Please call me as soon as you can. It's very important."

Would that work? Did Anthony ever call into his machine? Where in the world was he?

Yielding to Nemesis's pleas, she took him out, standing still and watching while he ran around the yard sniffing out the trail of a mouse or a squirrel. She knew that if he ever caught one, he'd toy with it or bite off its head. Nemesis wasn't a guard cat, but he was a hunter. She placed him in the middle of the food chain, predator and prey. If she weren't so damn protective, she'd go inside and let him kill or be killed. At this time of year when the sun was low in the sky, it entered her eyes at an angle that was almost painful. She had to put her hand beside her face and shade her eyes to see Nemesis. The phone rang. She might have gone in to answer it, but she stayed outside and watched her cat. When he got tired and hungry, they went back in.

There was no message on the answering machine. Unavailable, call screening said.

The first thing she did when she reached her office on Monday was to compare the Burke P. Lovell she had typed on the ancient Corona to the Burke P. Lovell on Mariah's birth certificate. She found that they were not a match. Next she called Janet Randall and asked if anyone else had inquired about the deed to the ranch or Benjamin deWitt's *History of the Blue.*

"Only you," Janet said.

She thought of calling the librarian in Las Vegas to see if she had told anyone else that Anthony Barbour had purchased the history, but she doubted it would prove anything. Anthony was a tumbleweed, and he could have told anyone anywhere that he had the book, if he still had the book.

Then she called Rachel and left a message. When Rachel showed up about an hour later, her cheeks were flushed with excitement. "Have I got a lot to tell you," she said.

"I've got a lot to tell you."

"You first."

Claire told Rachel about her visit to Reserve, her attempts to locate a copy of the history and all she had learned about the death of Ellen deWitt.

Rachel was skeptical. "You think someone would kill to get a copy of a book?"

"Maybe they didn't intend to kill. If a thief is armed and surprised in the act, anything can happen."

"I'll call the sheriff in Globe and see what I can find out."

"Good."

It was Rachel's turn. "The description you gave me of the woman you saw Gail talking to resembled Lisa Cook, a student we've suspected of selling drugs. She shaved her head after she broke up with her boyfriend, and since then she's been wearing a black baseball cap. We never saw her meet up with Gail, but we did see her closing a drug deal over the weekend and we arrested her. As soon as we threatened to call her parents, she confessed and snitched on her customers. Gail Benton was one of them. Lisa was supplying her with Percocet. You were right about that. Lisa says she stopped selling to Gail because she owed her money."

"If Gail had stolen the books, she'd have money by now."

"Unless she owed it to someone else." Gail was a bone Rachel was still unwilling to relinquish. "Have you heard whether Rex Barker is driving a new truck?"

"He wasn't the last time I saw him."

"I'll let you know what I find out in Globe."

"Thanks," Claire said.

Rachel went back to her office, and Claire began calling antiquarian bookstores to see if anyone had heard from Anthony Barbour. Great Expectations in Tucson hadn't seen him. Yestermorrow in Scottsdale hadn't heard from him in aeons. It had been a long time for Book Cellar in Denver, too. On her fourth call, however, Claire produced a lead. Sam Downey at Country Road Books in Durango had heard that Anthony was on his way to Santa Fe to see Joan Winn. Claire felt as if she'd turned over an ace. Since this call had been her lucky charm, Claire also asked if Sam had seen Rex Barker recently.

"He was in last week," he replied.

"How is he?"

"Same old Rex."

"Still driving his Silverado?"

"Still driving it. One of these days that junker will leave Rex stranded beside the highway."

"He'll stick out his thumb, and a woman will pick him up."

"Shame he can't afford to buy a new truck. He should have held on to more copies of his own book. It's worth more as a collector's item than it ever was as a reader's item."

"Rex probably has a box stored in his basement waiting for the price to go up. He's a poker player."

"Good luck finding Anthony Barbour."

"Thanks."

Next Claire called Joan Winn, the woman who had bought John Harlan's store in Santa Fe. She was a retired teacher who had refinanced her house to pay for the store. Fortunately, she had her pension to keep the lean times from turning into the lien times. "How have you been, Claire?" Joan Winn asked. "Are you liking your new job?"

"It has been more exciting than I ever would have imagined," Claire said.

"Good excitement or bad?"

"Both. I've been trying to get in touch with Anthony Barbour, but he hasn't been returning my calls."

"Does he ever return calls?"

"Not since I've known him. Sam Downey told me you're expecting him."

"On Thursday."

"So he's still alive."

"Do you have any reason to think otherwise?"

"Not really. Did he say what time on Thursday?"

"Are you kidding? Getting Anthony to commit to a time is like asking Bill Clinton to keep his zipper zipped."

"How do you know it will be Thursday?"

"Because I'm holding a book that he wants badly, and I told him if he doesn't pick it up by then, I'm selling it to another buyer."

"I'll be up on Thursday. If he gets there before I do, stick his feet in a bucket of wet cement."

"I'll try. Did you ever get Burke Lovell's books back?"

"Most of them," Claire said.

"That must have been a relief."

"In some ways it was."

Rachel called later in the morning. "The police in Globe told me they have no suspects in the deWitt murder and robbery," she said. "It had the MO of a teen punk burglary, only someone got killed. The back door was jimmied open. They took a TV, a VCR, stuffed the pillowcases with costume jewelry, the usual stuff. Either they were your basic stupid thief or doing a good imitation. The one thing unusual was that this was the only robbery reported in Globe that month, and they tend to occur in a series. But this might have been the first, and the murder scared the burglars into ceasing and desisting. The police got a couple of prints, but they haven't been able to trace them."

"I got a lead on the missing history," Claire said. "The only person I know who has one will be in Santa Fe on Thursday. I'm going up there."

"Good luck," Rachel said.

When she got off the phone with Rachel, Claire went to the

kitchen for a cup of coffee, passing Gail's office en route. After she looked through the window and saw a dark computer screen and a dark room, she stopped in to see Ruth.

"Is Gail out?" she asked.

"She called in sick. Some lingering problem from the accident. I recommended a chiropractor, and I'm going to take her over there this afternoon."

"Is she still having car problems?"

"Yes."

"She ought to buy a new one."

"She can't afford it," Ruth said. She focused her keen eyes on Claire. "You're looking good. Have you changed your hairdo? Your makeup?"

"No."

"You haven't fallen in love, have you?"

"No," Claire said again. She had fallen into danger, however, which was raising her adrenaline level. Her senses were heightened. She was eating and sleeping less—hearing and seeing more. On the way back to her office, she stopped at the bathroom and looked at herself in the mirror. Her cheeks were flushed and her eyes were bright, even her hair seemed to have more body. She didn't need the coffee she was holding in her hand, and she emptied it down the drain.

On Thursday, she began her day by repulsing the monkey, embracing the tiger, feeding the cat, and locking the house tight. She wanted to be at Joan Winn's the minute she opened for business, which put her into commuter traffic on the interstate. She remembered when the road from Albuquerque to Santa Fe was a pleasant drive, and you could contemplate the scenery instead of gripping the steering wheel tight and seeing an angry face in your rearview mirror. These days I-25 was filled with determined people driving from Albuquerque to their state jobs in Santa Fe and equally determined people driving from Santa Fe to their executive jobs in Albuquerque. The speed limit was seventy-five, but no matter how fast you went, you were always tailgated.

Claire thought about Anthony on the drive north. He was good company whenever you saw him, but you only saw him when it suited him. Anthony lived life on his terms. You could take them, or you could leave them. He was a man who'd break the heart of anyone foolish enough to give it to him. Anthony had given up a lot to pursue his footloose lifestyle—money, pets, security, close relationships—yet it was a lifestyle other people envied. Sometimes his life made no sense to Claire, sometimes it annoyed her. But today, battling the traffic on the interstate, she understood how it might appeal to anyone who had to make this drive every morning and every night and spend the hours in between confined to an office cubicle.

She got off the interstate at St. Francis and circled downtown on Paseo de Peralta, noticing a falcon sculpture she admired on the wall of the Gerald Peters Gallery. When she reached Canyon Road, she turned right and drove a few blocks to Winn Books. Joan Winn was turning the key in the lock as Claire pulled into the parking lot.

"You're here bright and early," she said when Claire entered the store.

The sunlight beamed through the window, spotlighting a threadbare Oriental rug, highlighting the antique maps on the walls and the shelves of leather-bound books. Joan Winn had tidied up the store and made it a lot more orderly than it was when John was the proprietor. There was a sense of serenity and stability here that appealed to Claire.

"I always feel so comfortable here," she said.

Joan was a plump woman with thick brown hair that she wore in a knot on top of her head. The reading glasses that she purchased in the five-and-dime sat low on her nose. She pushed up the sleeves of her sweater and put her hands down on the counter. "I hope I can continue," she said. "I'm afraid the day is coming when we'll be downloading everything we read from the Internet, and books will be like fine handcrafted furniture. What there is will be choice, but there will be less and less of it." Joan had been a teacher for twenty-five years, and she had a tendency to lecture. She picked up a spray bottle and began to clean the glass-topped counter, giving Claire the impression it would be an intrusion to sit around waiting for Anthony to show up.

"Are the galleries open yet?" she asked.

Joan looked at her watch. "If they're not, they will be soon."

"I'll take a look while we're waiting for Anthony."

"Check in every hour or so. I should be able to hold him for that long."

"He knows that it's very important we get together."

"I'll remind him."

Claire began her gallery hopping by walking down Canyon Road, visiting three before checking back in with Joan, who was showing a customer a book. She looked at Claire over her glasses and said, "Not yet."

Claire went back to Canyon Road and walked uphill until she reached the Reginald Arnold Gallery, which was having an exhibit of black-and-white photographs by George Capo, consisting mostly of clouds. When Claire opened the door, the sound of a tinkling bell caused a pencil-thin young woman who sat at a desk working the phone, to lift her hand in a desultory wave. Her name was Jennifer Owen, a plaque on the desk said. The wave was sufficient greeting for Claire, who was content to be ignored while she worked her way through the striking photographs. Capo's blacks were dark and mysterious, his whites were dazzling. The subtle and luminous grays reminded Claire of Ansel Adams's theory that the world could be represented in nine zones of gray. Capo's clouds had the quality of a Rorschach test on which the viewer could project her own images. A series of three clouds—flying saucers in one photo— became an eagle with outstretched talons in the next. Claire hadn't seen a black-and-white exhibit for some time, and she had forgotten how evocative pure light and shadow could be. Her pleasure resembled the pleasure she took in reading, when she brought her own colors to the black-and-white letters on the page. What you got out of an exhibit like this depended on what you put in.

Jennifer was preoccupied with discussing her dinner plans. Santacafé? Geronimo's? There was a partition behind her, and beyond that the exhibit continued into another room. Claire worked her way to the back of the gallery, contemplating the clouds with Jennifer's conversation as background music. At the rear of the building an open door revealed an office with a desk and a work-table used to mount and frame art. Claire glanced in and saw an Ansel Adams print of the Ranchos de Taos Church lying on the table waiting to be framed. She entered the room and found three more prints from the Austin/Adams folio lying on the table. These prints were so rare that they almost had to be the ones that were stolen from her truck. Razored out of the folio, Claire thought, and rather skillfully, too. The razored edge was as smooth as glass. She felt as if she'd been punched in the stomach.

"Exquisite, aren't they?" Jennifer was suddenly at her elbow. Claire had been so engrossed in her discovery that she hadn't heard her approach.

"Aren't they?" She found herself parroting Jennifer. For a moment she was at a loss for words, then she asked, "Where did you get them?"

"Reginald bought them from a client who was settling an estate."

"What client? Do you know?"

"No." Prompted by the agitated tone of Claire's voice, a door closed tight behind Jennifer's carefully made-up eyes.

"A copy of the Austin/Adams folio was stolen from my truck."

"Your . . . truck?" Claire felt she was being ridiculed, and she wondered why. Because she was older? Because she wasn't skinny as a stick and dressed in Santa Fe black? Because she drove a truck? Maybe Jennifer hadn't been in New Mexico long enough to know that in this state it was considered chic to drive a truck, especially when you had no use for one.

"My truck," Claire repeated. She was tempted to pull out her business card to establish authority, but resisted the urge to prove herself to Jennifer Owen.

"I'm sure you're mistaken. Reginald would not buy stolen art-work," Jennifer replied, stepping between Claire and the prints.

Claire suspected that not only did Reginald Arnold buy stolen artwork, he knowingly bought it. He was one of the first dealers she had called when she discovered the Austin/Adams portfolio was missing. He should have called her back the moment he saw these prints. "Did he check the provenance when he bought the prints?" she asked. The provenance would show the trail of ownership and reveal whether or not a work of art had been stolen.

"Of course," Jennifer replied. "This is a private room. You have no right to be in here." She guided Claire to the door and closed it behind them.

Claire felt drained enough to allow herself to be led back into the gallery. Provenances were all too easy to fake by a seller or a buyer, she knew. Even easier if both were in collusion. If the prints had been stolen in one state and sold in another, it would be interstate commerce and the FBI might get involved. But in this case they had been moved from one part of the state to another. Rachel's authority didn't extend this far, and Claire didn't hold out much hope for the Santa Fe police, who were more concerned with rape and murder than they were with fine art photography. By the time they got here, the prints would be long gone. The Arnold Gallery must have been mounting and framing them for a customer. She doubted that even Reginald Arnold would be arrogant enough to display stolen prints on his gallery wall.

"Are you all right?" Jennifer turned condescendingly solicitous. "Can I get you a glass of water? Would you like to sit down?"

What Claire really wanted to do was go outside and get some fresh air, but she had a few more questions. "Have you ever met a woman named Samantha Lovell?"

"No." Jennifer pursed her lips, which were tinted brown to match her eye shadow.

"How about the artist, Rusty Siler?"

Jennifer sniffed. "Never heard of him," she said, but she paused just long enough to make Claire wonder if she was telling the truth. "Why don't you leave your card, and I'll have Reginald call you?"

"I'll call him," Claire said. The bell tinkled as she stepped into the street. Santa Fe was always ten degrees colder than Albuquerque, but Claire had neglected to prepare herself by bringing a hat or gloves. She turned up her collar and inserted her hands in her pockets. The air smelled of smoke. She knew it was only piñon firewood burning, but it smelled as if the City Different was on fire. The smell of piñon was considered one of Santa Fe's charms. But charm had become a commodity here, a card to be dealt in the relentless pursuit of status and power. To Claire, seeking prestige resembled attending a cocktail party full of well-dressed people smoking and drinking in a room lined with mirrors. All you got was a reflection of your reflection reflected in someone else's eyes. Why, she wondered, did people care so much about something that was basically just mirrors and smoke?

When she got back to Winn Books, Anthony Barbour stood beside the counter talking to Joan. He was a slight person with a long brown beard that appeared to have been shaped by the wind. He wore a tweed coat that was thrift store shabby and a knitted cap pulled down over his ears. The tattered hem of his jeans peeked out from under the coat. When he gave Claire a hug, he had the reassuring smell of tobacco and wool.

"You're cold," he said.

"Very," she replied.

"You'll be happy to know that I have your book. I was coming to Albuquerque tomorrow to give it to you."

"I'll take it now," she said, knowing that in Anthony's world there was often a gap between outcome and intent.

"It's in the van. Are you going to explain why this book is so important to you?" he asked.

"I am," she said, but she didn't intend to do it in front of Joan Winn, who was standing behind the counter burning with curiosity.

"What book are you talking about?" she asked. Her eyes were bright and inquisitive as she peered over the top of her dime-store glasses.

"You're better off not knowing," Claire replied.

CHAPTER FIFTEEN

Anthony picked up the book he had purchased from Joan, then he and Claire went outside to his VW van, which he'd parked in the lot behind the store. There was a cracked and faded peace sign decal in the window, a faint signal from the tumultuous past. To his regret, Anthony had been born too late to be a hippie—he spent the sixties in diapers and in grammar school—but it was a time he felt connected to, and fantasized about. Fantasy was always a factor in Anthony's life. There were pockets in the Southwest where the sixties never died, and Anthony sought them out, asking his elders to tell him about love beads and drugs. He pulled the handle on the van's side door, and it rumbled open with a sound that took Claire back to 1968, Morocco and Pietro. They had traveled through southern Europe and northern Africa in a van that looked just like this one and broke down in every country they visited. Claire still had a vivid recollection of the gang of dirty boys in Bershid, Morocco, who carried the engine from the van to the garage. She wondered how many hundreds of thousands of miles were on Anthony's van, how many new engines had been installed. She and Pietro had lived in the back of his van, but every square inch of this one was taken up with boxes of books. Tufts of gold shag carpeting sprouted in the spaces between the boxes. Claire despaired of ever finding any particular book in this mess. How could Anthony even know what he had, much less where it was? He lifted out three boxes and placed them carefully on the ground. He opened the fourth, and there, at the top, was a copy of Benjamin deWitt's *The History of the Blue*.

"Now are you going to tell me what is so important about this book?" Anthony asked. "I'd be lucky if I could sell it for ten dollars."

"I need to look at it first." Claire picked up the history, balancing it in her hands with the reverence she showed any book. The binding on Benjamin deWitt's *History of the Blue* was loose, the cover was a faded and scuffed green, the endpapers were dirty. The poor condition could be expected to reduce the price of any book, but this one defied expectations. Claire looked for the library stamp that would decrease the value even further, but she didn't find one. She wondered how something that appeared so drab and ordinary could have caused so much trouble. Could this beat-up volume possibly be the solution to a disturbing mystery? Could someone really have been murdered over this brown bird of a book? She began turning the pages.

"Are you going to read it right here now?" Anthony asked.

"If I have to."

"Be my guest." He opened the door on the passenger's side of the cab, made a bow, and motioned Claire in. "I've got all day."

There was a boxful of yellow wrappers from McDonald's and a *Santa Fe Reporter* lying on the passenger's seat. Anthony picked them up, brushed the crumbs from the upholstery, and Claire sat down. The smell of moldy carpet, dusty books, and time warp made her sneeze. As Anthony walked around the van, she flipped through deWitt's *History of the Blue* to see if any phrase or name caught her eye. The Stoner name was mentioned frequently, which didn't surprise her—she already knew the Stoners had been in the Blue for generations—but nothing else captured her attention.

Anthony swung the tail of his coat out of his way and sat down in the driver's seat, which had a cover made out of wooden beads.

Claire skimmed through the book, discovering little except that Ben deWitt was a plodding writer. She returned to the beginning and examined the title page and the copyright page. There was no inscription on the title page. Since the book had been printed after the death of the author, discovering anything in Ben's writing could be considered a message from the grave. It wasn't what Claire expected to find, and it wasn't in Ben's writing, but the message was there in the dedication. She read it once to herself and once again out loud to Anthony.

"'This book is dedicated to my amanuensis Kathleen Geraty; to the light of my life, our daughter Mariah, and to my friend in time of need Burke P. Lovell.' That explains it," Claire said.

Anthony swiveled the steering wheel, which was wrapped in strips of leather that were coming unsewn. "Explains what?"

"Mariah Geraty is the daughter of Benjamin deWitt, not Burke Lovell. Burke had this book printed after Ben died, so he must have read this."

"So?"

"Burke left the ranch to Mariah. The family is trying to have his will overturned on the grounds that Mariah deceived him by pretending to be his daughter. The dedication proves he knew what he was doing, and he knew Mariah wasn't his daughter. The book will make it a lot harder—if not impossible—for the family to gain control of the ranch."

"He told everybody she was his daughter."

"But he didn't say so in his will, only that he was leaving the property to Mariah Geraty. Unless the family can prove deception on Mariah's part or incapacity on Burke's, Mariah gets the property."

"Does Mariah believe she is his daughter?"

"Yes."

"I never understood the guy," Anthony said. "Why did he pretend he was Mariah's father? He was a Ph.D. and a university administrator. Why did he live on that redneck river with all those ranchers on the BLM dole?"

"It's a beautiful area."

Anthony shrugged. "I drive through beautiful areas all the time. It doesn't mean I'd want to live in one," he said in his soft voice that had a tendency to get lost in his beard. Claire had to lean forward to hear him answer his own question. "Maybe Burke let Mariah think she was his daughter because he wanted her to stick around. He'd be selfish enough to do something like that. I went out there one weekend to sell him some books, and I met her. She's young. She's beautiful. She can ride. She's got a kid. If you were Burke, wouldn't you rather have her for support than Corinne, who's too screwed up to leave the house? Mariah helped Burke die, right?"

"Right."

"If you were Mariah, wouldn't you rather believe Burke was your father than that ne'er-do-well Ben deWitt?"

"Apparently Mariah showed up at the ranch with a birth certificate that had been doctored to say Burke was her father."

"Doctored by who?"

"Possibly the mother, who would have wanted Mariah to have the ranch and apparently had no love left for Ben deWitt. Maybe the birth certificate was her message from the grave."

"Well, if Mariah is Ben deWitt's daughter, she's entitled to the place. Ranches are supposed to stay in families forever in the Blue, aren't they? Ben probably just considered Burke a caretaker until his own heir grew up."

"Burke left his stamp on it by insisting that it be a nature preserve."

"If Burke's children got it, they'd sell it in a minute and blow the money. Do they know Mariah's not his daughter?"

"If they have a copy of this book, they have evidence. But for them, it's a two-edged sword—proof that Mariah wasn't Burke's daughter, but also proof that he knew it." She held up the history for Anthony to see. "Someone—quite possibly a family member—will do anything to get this book. That's why I've been trying to get ahold of you."

"Sorry," Anthony said, giving the steering wheel a spin and mumbling into his beard. "I meant to call you."

"Burke's copy was stolen from my truck, and copies are missing from libraries all over the Southwest and from Page One, Too."

"It had to have a very small print run."

"Thirty copies, Lola Falter told me."

"It wouldn't be hard to steal them all. You should be grateful that I'm so difficult to locate, or else mine might be gone, too."

"I was worried about you, Anthony. Ben deWitt's sister was killed in a robbery of her house in Globe last month, and her copy is also missing."

"Now that you have it, how do you intend to protect yourself?"

"I don't know."

"Who do you think is the thief?"

"Until I knew what the book said, I thought Mariah was a possibility."

"I never would have suspected her; she's too beautiful." Anthony tugged wisfully at his beard and stared out the window, a scruffy man fantasizing about a beautiful woman. "Did Burke leave that book on the shelf for everybody to see?"

"It was there, but it was mis-shelved. Hidden by Burke, possibly, or by someone else. Anyone who knew Burke would have expected it to be in place, and might have assumed it was missing."

"Who knew you had one to steal?"

"James was in the room when I packed it."

"He's a possibility. He has a history of mental problems, and he's got a shark for a wife. They were there the weekend I was. Charming couple. Corinne? She's weird enough, and she'd hate to give up the house. It could have been any of them, or it could have been all of them."

"The Stoners told me that Samantha and James agreed to sell the ranch to them if they got control of it."

"The Stoners are the neighboring ranchers?"

"Right."

"How was deWitt's sister killed?"

"She was shot."

"There you go. That's the way ranchers like to settle disagreements, with a bullet through the head." The sun, beating in the window, began warming up the van. Claire rolled down her window.

"She was shot with a thirty-eight. I only saw rifles when I was at their ranch."

"That doesn't mean they don't have a thirty-eight. You know, solving this crime could be more fun than scouting books." Anthony had the bright-eyed expression of a coyote on the trail of a rabbit or a book scout on the trail of a sought-after book. Claire didn't expect his enthusiasm to last forever—Anthony had a short attention span—but she intended to take advantage of it while it did.

"The Austin/Adams folio was also stolen from my truck."

"Was it in good condition?"

"Excellent."

"Those are harder than hell to find. I don't know if I've ever seen one that wasn't under lock and key in a university's rare-book room."

"I came across some of the prints today in the Reginald Arnold Gallery. The woman who works there claims she doesn't know Samantha Lovell or her boyfriend, Rusty Siler, but I'm not sure I believe her."

"You don't think Samantha was involved," Anthony scoffed, getting a wistful look again.

"Why not? Because she's good-looking?" Claire knew all too well that pretty women were capable of vicious acts, but Anthony didn't want to admit it.

"Samantha buys books from me now and then. She drives a hard bargain, but she wouldn't kill anybody."

"Why does she buy from you? She's not a collector, is she?"

"No, but she knows some wealthy collectors here. I sell to her at a dealer's discount. She sells to the collectors at market value and makes herself some money."

"So she knows something about the rare-book trade," Claire said, thinking of the trouble that could have been avoided if only Anthony had answered his phone. "I suppose she knows how to buy and sell on the Internet."

"Why not? Everybody else does. I've even gotten an e-mail address myself. Maybe someday I'll give up my van and get a Web site, only then I'd have to stay home more." Anthony squirmed on his beaded seat cover and spun the steering wheel with the palm of his hand.

"I found what I believe to be the stolen prints on Canyon Road. Rusty's an artist. Rusty and Samantha both live here."

"Stolen objects go to the market, and this is where the market is," Anthony insisted.

"If you think I'm wrong, you could prove it by helping me catch the thief. Are you interested?"

"Sure."

"Could you come to Albuquerque for a couple of days? I'll put you up in my guest room."

"Okay," Anthony said. "I'll follow you."

"All right." Claire would have preferred to follow Anthony to make sure he didn't pull off the interstate somewhere and disappear, but it made more sense for her to lead, since she knew exactly where they were going.

They got in their respective vehicles and drove down Canyon Road, taking Paseo de Peralta to St. Francis to the interstate, with Anthony sticking close in the traffic. But once they got on I-25, he began to drift. Claire watched the VW van in her rearview mirror lumbering along behind her like a truncated elephant. She felt as if she were tethered to the van, but the rope had a reverse pull, which let Anthony set the pace. He drove the interstate the way a trucker does, creeping up the hills, speeding going down. When he slowed down, Claire slowed down. When he speeded up, she did, too. By the time they reached Albuquerque an hour later, she had a crick in her neck from looking backward. She got off the interstate at Central and led Anthony to the visitor's lot at the university.

She parked her truck there, too, and walked him to her office, where she dialed Rachel's number. While she was on the phone, Harrison walked by her window, stared at Anthony, and scowled. Rachel arrived in a few minutes, and when she entered the office, Anthony stood up and straightened his beard, getting wistful over another pretty woman. For a moment Claire thought they might be attracted to each other, but she dismissed the thought. Although they weren't that far apart in age, they lived in different generations. Rachel looked ahead. Anthony looked back. Rachel was a realist. Anthony was a dreamer. Rachel was neat. Anthony was sloppy. Rachel was courteous when she spoke to him, but she seemed to be looking at a point to the side of his face and above his shoulder rather than into his eyes. Claire suspected she considered Anthony too scruffy to be credible.

She told Rachel what she had discovered in Santa Fe, and showed her *The History of the Blue.*

Rachel stared at the book. "This is what all the fuss is about?"

"That's it," Claire replied.

"Not very impressive, is it?"

"Not very."

"Do you think the gallery owner will admit he bought stolen prints? Most likely those prints will be gone long before law enforcement gets there. I can't arrest anybody based on the evidence we have."

"Would you be willing to set up another sting?" Claire asked.

"I might."

Claire laid out the plan she had developed on the drive from Santa Fe, which involved Anthony finding a computer that would let him access his e-mail account, then e-mailing Five Numbers at anon.net.fi and offering to sell *The History of the Blue.*

"Won't Five Numbers wonder how Anthony got the e-mail address?" Rachel asked.

"Who ever it is will figure it came from me or John Harlan or Rex Barker or some other dealer Five Numbers tried to sell the books to. She—or he—is likely to go ahead anyway, being in too deep to get out now. In my opinion that book represents the ranch to the thief. You'd have to arrange to meet in some remote place," Claire said to Anthony.

"I'm game," Anthony said.

"Whoever it is has robbed a couple of times and killed once that we know of," Rachel said. This time she did look at Anthony. Their eyes met, and Claire saw that, whatever their differences, they shared a taste for adventure and for bringing this adventure to a successful conclusion. The three of them were an unlikely trio, but she felt they could pull it off.

"You'll have to find a spot in Albuquerque for the university police to get involved."

Claire had thought that through, too. "What about the West Mesa?" she asked. It was Albuquerque's open-air shooting gallery, the land of tumbleweed and rabbits, where fathers taught their sons to shoot, drug deals went down, and stolen cars and dead bodies turned up. Parts of it were within the city limits, and Rachel could operate there without a jurisdictional conflict.

"I know the spot," Rachel said. "I caught some students dealing Rohypnol there last year. Who's your e-mail server?" she asked Anthony.

"AOL," he mumbled into his beard, suggesting he was embarrassed to admit he had the crass and commercial server. "It makes it easy to check my messages while I'm traveling."

"Is that who you use?" Rachel asked Claire.

"Yes."

"All right. You two get together, send Five Numbers a message, and we'll take it from there." She stood up, brushed an imaginary wrinkle from her uniform, and shook Anthony's outstretched hand.

He spent the afternoon visiting rare-book dealers in town while Claire worked at the library. Harrison passed by her office again, stuck his head in the door, and asked if she intended to buy any books from Anthony Barbour.

"He has a copy of deWitt's *History of the Blue,*" Claire replied.

"Do we *need* that book?"

"It would round out Burke's collection." So would the Adams prints, but Claire wasn't ready to mention them yet. She wasn't ready to mention the sting yet, either, hoping that in a few days she'd have better news.

"Is there money in the budget for another purchase?" Harrison asked.

"There's enough for this one," Claire replied.

When she got home that night, she let out the cat, watched him run around the yard, and calculated when she ought to start worrying about Anthony Barbour showing up. She had invited him for dinner, and he said he would come. He hadn't asked what time. She hadn't wanted to appear uptight by suggesting one. Anthony was a vegetarian, and she intended to cook a frozen pasta dinner, since she wouldn't need to start it until he walked in the door. She considered dinner time to be six o'clock, but this was New Mexico. Calculations made elsewhere didn't apply here, and she had tired of being the first person at every party, so she automatically added an hour to most plans. Anthony being Anthony, she added another hour and decided dinner would be at eight. By seven she had fed the cat and watched the news, which featured a terrible crime that had taken place on the Rio Grande Bridge in Taos.

Claire began to pace back and forth across the gray Berber carpet that ran from one end of her house to the other, imagining the Rio Grande Bridge as a metaphor for life. Six hundred feet below it, the river curved through the gorge like a ribbon thrown down by a cavalier god. The Rio Grande could be gray and brooding, blue and sparkling, muddy and turbulent, but when the light hit just right, it turned into a ribbon of gold. The river's banks were littered with the detritus of dumb mistakes: the air force jet that, on a dare, a pilot had flown successfully under the bridge only to hit a power line on the way back up; the RV that had been left in neutral with the emergency brake off; the canoes that had attempted to run the rapids. On the news she'd learned that a teenage boy had been thrown off the bridge by two other teenagers who wanted his car. Even in New Mexico, where people got killed over cars often enough, it was a horrific crime. While she paced, Claire wondered what it was that gave this particular crime such impact. The depth of the plunge and the length of time it would take for the victim to reach the bottom while fully aware of what was coming next? Or did the gorge represent some fear residing deep in the collective subconscious?

Claire pondered how people she knew would approach the bridge. She saw herself as walking within a few feet of the railing, then pulling back. Harrison would stare at the bridge, but never attempt to put a foot on it. Evan would stride across, full of purpose, looking neither to the left or right until the minute he jumped off. She didn't see Anthony on the bridge at all but as skirting the edge of the cliff, flirting with the abyss. As far as she knew, Anthony had no safety net. Was she worried that something had happened to him? Claire asked herself. That he had changed his mind? Or was she just a person who was chained to the clock?

She checked the time again as she passed through the kitchen, saw that it was now a quarter to eight, and decided to boil water hoping that would produce Anthony even though her mother's adage that a watched pot won't boil could easily be translated into a person who is waited for too eagerly will never show up. The water brought her luck, however, because as soon as she turned on the faucet, the doorbell rang.

Anthony stood on the stoop in his long coat, wearing his pack on his back. "Am I late?" he asked.

"I was just putting on some water to boil for pasta."

"I ran into Joe Carnright, and we went out for a drink."

Long drink, she thought, but she didn't say it. She led Anthony to the guest room to deposit his coat and backpack, then into the kitchen, where Nemesis was curled up in a chair. "Nice house," Anthony said. "Nice cat." He picked up Nemesis, who began to purr.

The water boiled quickly, the pasta cooked in a few minutes, and they sat down to eat. This was the first time Claire had a man who wasn't a relative to dinner in this house. Anthony was too old to be a son, too young to be a lover; he existed in a kind of no-man's-land as far as Claire was concerned. Still, he added some sparkle to the dinner table, although all they talked about was books.

After dinner they went to the den, and Anthony logged on to AOL as a visitor, using his own address and password.

"Is there any way for Five Numbers to tell that this message is coming from Albuquerque and not from your house?" Claire asked.

"There might be," Anthony replied. "If he read all the boiler plate at the bottom of the message. Let's hope the thief is too impatient or too stupid for that."

"You'll be more believable if you set a high price. Then your motive will appear to be money."

"Whatever the price, once I sell it, I'm a witness and a threat. James or that redneck rancher or whoever shows up could take the book away, then take me out."

"The university police will be there."

"Do you trust them?"

"Rachel set up a sting at Page One, Too, and she handled it well."

"Were any weapons drawn?"

"No. The thief didn't even show up. If you don't want to do this, Anthony, I'll understand. No book is worth getting shot over."

"Do *you* want to call it off?"

"No," Claire admitted.

"Are you afraid?"

"No. I'm angry."

"Then, let's do it." He was excited, Claire suspected, as excited as she was and curious, too. The need for danger could be as much a part of human nature as the need for sex and security, only the proportions were likely to change as one grew older. Claire wondered if she sought excitement now because she'd had so little in the BDE—before divorcing Evan—years.

Anthony clicked the "write" icon. "What's the address?"

"It came from an anonymous server in Finland, 26688@anon. net.fi."

"What do we say?"

"You heard someone has been looking for the history, and you have one. Set a high price."

Anthony's fingers pecked at the keys. "A thousand dollars?"

"That's good. Say you're in Arizona, but you're leaving for New Mexico early tomorrow morning. You need to hear back before you leave."

Anthony typed in the message. "What happens next?" he asked.

"We wait to see if we get a response."

Anthony clicked the send icon, got out of AOL, and yawned. He was a man who could go from high excitement to total exhaustion in a manner of minutes. "Time to go to bed," he said. The word "bed" hung in the air like a particle of dust in a beam of afternoon sunlight until he added, "I'm in the guest room, right?"

"That's right."

"See you in the morning."

Anthony went through the door to his room, and Claire went through the door to hers. For her it took hours for sleep to replace excitement. While she tossed and turned, she considered the suspects. To her the book-dealing connection and the art world connection said Samantha, but it was also what she wanted to believe.

Anthony was up before she was checking his messages on the computer. By the time Claire awoke, it was eight-thirty. If she didn't hurry, she'd be late for work. Anthony had printed the messages from Five Numbers and was sitting at her kitchen table drinking coffee. He handed Claire the printouts. The first one read, "Your price is too high."

"Take it or leave it," Anthony had replied. Claire was glad she'd been asleep when he'd written that one. It was closer to losing the deal than she cared to get.

"I'll take it," Five Numbers answered.

"What do we do now?" Anthony asked Claire.

"Say you need the money today."

They picked up their coffees, went into the den, and sat down in front of the computer, where Anthony pecked out a response and sent it into cyber space. "I need the money today. Cash."

"Makes me sound like a junkie," he said to Claire.

"A book junkie."

They sipped their coffee and stared at the screen while they waited for the messages to circle the globe from Albuquerque to Finland to somewhere in the Southwest and back again.

"You have mail," the AOL voice eventually said. Anthony clicked on the mail icon.

"Where in New Mexico are you?" Five Numbers asked.

"Albuquerque," Anthony answered.

"Meet me in the plaza in Old Town at five o'clock," the message came back.

"I'll meet you on the West Mesa. A thousand dollars cash, and the book is yours." Anthony typed out the directions Rachel had provided.

Several minutes later the answer came back from Five Numbers. "The money will be there," it said.

CHAPTER SIXTEEN

Rachel's backup for the sting was a university policeman named Paul Teague. He had the short hair and clean-cut good looks of a Mormon missionary and appeared to be the same age as Rachel—mid-twenties. Nineteen had been proven to be the optimum age for a soldier. Claire wondered if mid-twenties was the optimum age for a cop.

They met in the Route 66 Diner on Central. Two police officers in the glass bowl of Claire's office would have sent up a red flag to her coworkers. Claire had found a book that was the same size as the history, and she wrapped it in brown paper. The real history was locked up in the center's safe; it had become far too valuable to risk losing. Anthony surprised her by showing up at the diner on time, proving that he could do it when he had to. Paul and Rachel wore their uniforms and were armed. Anthony wore his long tweed coat.

"You've got a big responsibility," Paul said when they were introduced. "Are you up for it?"

"Sure," Anthony replied.

"You need to take off the coat when we get there," Rachel said. "I don't want anyone to think you're concealing a weapon."

"Whatever." Anthony shrugged.

He was the one who was taking the risk. Although he claimed that didn't concern him, he tugged at his beard a lot while he drove

Rachel and Claire to the West Mesa in his van. Paul followed in an unmarked university police car.

They took I-40 to Paseo del Volcan, the road that passed the volcano and led to a branch of the Bernalillo County Detention Center, the Double Eagle Airport, and the shooting range that catered to the public and the police. The signs for each of these places were shot full of holes by marksmen who couldn't wait to get to the range. It was wide-open country. Chamisa and sage rolled on and on like an unrippled sea, a surprisingly static landscape for a city where the vegetation varied with every change in elevation. At this time of year, the sage and chamisa were gray and dry as kindling. Occasionally the flatness was broken by a fence that became a backstop for tumbleweed or by a mound of broken rocks that had been tossed out by the volcano. The volcanic rocks were black and pockmarked, splattered with splashes of gold and orange lichen. The view looked into the monoliths of downtown and up at the Sandias, which were elephant-gray at this time of day.

Paul parked the police car at the airport and got in the van. Rachel directed Anthony down a rutted dirt road that followed a fence line. In places, the road had become too bumpy to drive, and a new road had been cut in a loop that swung wide of the old. They drove east until they went over a rise and could no longer see Paseo del Volcan. Rachel told Anthony to park beside a mound of volcanic rock. When they stepped out of the van, the ground was littered with shotgun casings and marked with the hieroglyphics of cowboy boots and running shoes. A paint can, upended on top of a fence post, was peppered with bullet holes. Ankle-deep indentations in the ground indicated a prairie dog colony lived here. A garbage bag had gotten impaled on a creosote bush.

Rachel looked at her watch and announced that it was three o'clock. She stood with her feet planted a few feet apart and her back to the view, making it clear that she was the one who was in charge of this operation. "I had two reasons to get here early," she said. "One is to make sure we have this area to ourselves. As you can see, it's a popular place for shooters. The van is tall enough to be seen from the road by anyone planning to consummate a drug deal or buy a book. Let's hope the drug dealers go away, and the book buyer doesn't. The second reason is that I want us to be ready. Claire, Paul, and I will conceal ourselves behind the mound. We won't be able to see anyone approach, but we'll hear them. Anthony, if you recognize the vehicle, signal that by stepping out of the van and closing the door. Be sure to activate the tape recorder first," she said, reminding him of the one she'd hidden in the van.

"All right."

She gave Anthony directions for revealing who the buyers were and whether they were armed. Anthony was thin as a reed and not very imposing in his T-shirt and jeans. Rachel wanted the buyer to consider him a harmless, ineffectual book scout and be duped into making an incriminating admission. There was nothing illegal about buying a book—even for an exorbitant price—so their case might rest on any admissions or threats the buyer made.

"It's not likely you'll get a perp to admit to killing anybody," Rachel said, "but you may get him or her or them to admit to stealing copies of the book. Collect the money, and when you hand over the book, say so."

"And in a voice we can hear," Paul added. "Don't mumble."

Anthony ignored him. "They'll want to examine the book. The minute they unwrap it, I'm in trouble."

"As soon as you collect the money, we'll appear. They'll be looking at the book, so we'll have surprise working for us."

"As far as they know, I'm all alone out here. What's to stop them from taking the book and keeping the money?" asked Anthony.

"We'll stop them. Are you ready?" Rachel asked.

"Ready," Anthony said.

"We need to conceal ourselves now. The buyer may show up early to check out the site."

Anthony climbed into the van. Claire looked back before they went behind the mound and saw him sitting in the driver's seat with his arm resting on the open window. Rachel knew exactly where to hide. When they sat down on the ground with their backs to the rock pile, Claire asked if she'd done this before. "Twice," Rachel said. "When I was with the APD. I did a lot of surveillance back then. It can be very boring. You have to train yourself to stay alert and to hold your water."

"Is that why you went to work for the university?"

"Part of it. There's a better class of criminal at UNM. Mostly what you get on the APD is mindless violence—fights, armed robbery, drug deals." She stretched out her legs, crossed her arms, and began listening for any sound that wasn't airplanes or wind, indicating that conversation had ended and surveillance had begun. Paul sat down beside her and followed her lead into a state of deep concentration.

Claire made herself as comfortable as she could and watched the sky where cumulonimbus clouds took on ominous shapes of mouths and claws and a vulture circled lazily. The plan that had seemed like a calculated risk in her office, was becoming a reckless long shot out here. The thought that they could be risking Anthony's life over a book made Claire very anxious. There was no way of knowing who would show up, how many would show up, how dangerous they would be. If Rachel and Paul hadn't looked so determined, she would have suggested calling the plan off.

She wondered what Anthony's thoughts were while he waited in the van. Two hours could be an eternity if you counted every passing minute. A cloud passed over the sun. A rabbit ran across the mesa, stared at them briefly, then darted away. She became aware of distant sounds, cars coming and going on Paseo del Volcan, dogs barking in the yards of houses down below. Occasionally voices or snatches of music reached her on the wind. The words were indistinct, but the music had a sixties beat, and she wondered if she was overhearing Anthony listening to his favorite tapes. Time passed, she became accustomed to the rhythm of the place and the music of the wind. She heard a vehicle come down the road, rattling its axle as it bumped across the ruts. Claire hoped Anthony had turned off his tape deck and turned on the tape recorder.

She looked at her watch—4:30. "The buyer is here early," she whispered. "If that's who it is."

"The perp might have wanted to get here first to set the scene," said Rachel.

Before the newly arrived vehicle even came to a stop, they heard the door of the van slide open and roll shut again, the prearranged signal that Anthony recognized the buyer. The faces of book dealers and Burke's heirs flashed through Claire's mind.

They heard the vehicle stop. Rachel and Paul got into crouches with their guns in their hands. Two doors opened and shut.

"Samantha?" they heard Anthony ask incredulously. "*You're* Five Numbers?" Although Claire had suspected Samantha, up until this moment the possibility existed that the thief was someone else, someone Claire didn't even know. That she'd been right didn't make her feel victorious. It made her feel sick.

"This has to be the first time in your life you've ever been early," Samantha said to Anthony.

"Am I? I hadn't noticed. I don't wear a watch. I did what I had to do in town and came over here." Anthony was enunciating clearly, maybe too clearly, Claire thought.

"What did you have to do?"

"Buy and sell books. Who's your friend?"

"This is Rusty." She didn't mention a last name. "How did you get my e-mail address?"

"A bookseller gave it to me and said if I had a *History of the Blue*, someone at 26688@anon.net.fi might be interested. I had no idea it would be you."

"What bookseller?"

"I promised not to tell."

"Why are you asking such a high price for a regional history?"

"I was told that someone at your address might be willing to pay. That's all I know. A thousand dollars would go a long way right now."

"Did you bring the book?" Rusty spoke for the first time. His voice had lost the ironic, mocking tone Claire had heard earlier and gained a hard edge.

"Yes. Did you bring the money with you?" The way he phrased that sentence was a signal that one of them—of both of them—could be armed. Claire tensed. Paul began to inch forward, but Rachel motioned for him to wait.

"We want to see the book first," Samantha said.

It was the point at which Anthony was supposed to hand over the book, signaling for Rachel and Paul to appear, but instead, he attempted to draw Samantha and Rusty out. "You haven't told me why you're willing to pay a thousand dollars for it," he said. Claire admired his daring, but Rusty's voice indicated he was irritated.

"Just give us the book," he demanded.

"What difference does it make?" Samantha asked. "You want the money, I want the book. A book's worth whatever price a buyer and seller agree on. Isn't that what you always say?"

"I just want to know. That's all. To satisfy my curiosity."

"It was important to my father. It's important to me."

"Important enough to steal and ruin your reputation for?"

"Give us the book," Rusty snapped.

"It's in the van. I'll get it."

"No, I'll get it," said Rusty. "Where exactly is it?"

"On the passenger's seat."

They heard the door open and shut. "Make sure it's the right book," Rusty said to Samantha, "and we're out of here."

No money had changed hands, and it wasn't the signal they'd been expecting, but the time had come for Rachel and Paul to act. They ran out from behind the mound with their weapons drawn.

Claire heard Rachel say, "Drop the gun, Rusty."

"You son of a bitch," Rusty said to Anthony. "You set us up."

"You set yourselves up," Anthony replied.

"This book isn't the history!" Samantha cried.

Claire had been ordered to conceal herself until Rusty and Samantha were disarmed. From where she hid, everyone seemed to be yelling in unison.

"Drop it," said Rachel. "You're under arrest."

"What for?" asked a surly Rusty.

"The theft of library books and the murder of Ellen deWitt."

"What kind of cops are you anyway?"

"UNM police."

"Jesus Christ, we're getting busted by the Keystone cops," Rusty said.

"Are you going to drop the weapon?" Rachel demanded.

"It's yours," Rusty said.

Rachel began reading the suspects their rights, which was the signal they'd been disarmed and it was safe for Claire to appear. She walked around the rock pile to see Paul handcuffing Rusty while Rachel kept her gun pointed at him.

Samantha's face was distorted in fear and in anger. A suede purse, trimmed with fringe, hung from her shoulder. Her hands, embellished by their silver rings, were clenched. "Claire! Did you have to get involved in this?"

"You took the university's books, Samantha."

"They should have been my books."

"You could have had them, if you'd wanted them."

"You're keeping the family from getting the ranch. Mariah is not my father's daughter. She has no right to it."

"She's Ben deWitt's daughter. Your father knew that when he left her the ranch. The history proves it. Ever since Burke died, you've been stealing the histories from libraries all over the Southwest so no one else would discover what you knew."

"Where's yours?"

"In a university safe."

"How could you do this to me, Claire?"

Claire was close enough now to see the tears in Samantha's eyes. She was tall, slim, blonde, and all too unpleasantly reminiscent of Melissa. Even for this occasion she'd worn makeup. Her mascara ran and made dark streaks on her cheeks. She'd reached the age where you create your own face, and the face she'd created was bitter and disappointed. Claire wondered if Anthony considered her pretty now.

Samantha slid her hand down her side and into her purse. Claire heard a click as she pulled it out holding a slim silvery object that gleamed in the sun. Samantha raised her hand and lunged at Claire. Their proximity left two options: to yield or to fight back. There was no time to flee. The move was so quick and unexpected that Claire's reaction came automatically, revealing her true nature better than deliberation ever would. In tai chi every action embraced its opposite. Warriors won because they knew their opponents better than their opponents knew them. If the opponent mounted an aggressive attack, the victim should yield. Claire dodged Samantha's raised arm and stepped quickly aside. When the force of Samantha's lunge encountered no resistance, she stumbled and fell on the ground, twisting her ankle in a prairie dog burrow. In a flash Rachel was standing over her with a drawn weapon. Paul knelt down, took the object out of Samantha's hands, and cuffed her.

"Nice work," Rachel said to Claire.

Paul examined the slim silver weapon. "What is it?" he asked.

"A blade cutter," Claire answered. "There's a snap-off razor blade inside. When you push the plastic knob, the razor extends. It's used to cut tape and open boxes or to razor plates out of valuable books."

"There's not much to it," Paul said. "But it's sharp enough to sever an artery."

Samantha's fringed purse had fallen off her shoulder and lay beside her on the ground. Rachel picked it up, took out a wad of bills, and counted them. "Your thousand dollars," she said to Anthony. "I'm afraid I'll have to hold it for evidence."

Anthony was staring down at Samantha with the crushed expression of someone who has seen a dream shattered. "You were right," he mumbled to Claire, burying his disappointment in his beard.

It was a victory that gave Claire no pleasure.

Rusty and Samantha were indicted for robbery and murder. Rusty's fingerprints matched the prints found at Ellen deWitt's house. Samantha's prints were found on the stolen books. She knew about deWitt's history and suspected it contained information that could affect the validity of the will. When the family read the will, and James revealed that Claire had packed the history in her box of valuable books, Samantha drove to Albuquerque and stole the box. Laura, James, Rusty, and the Stoners helped steal the rest of the histories and were indicted as coconspirators, but no evidence could be found linking Corinne.

"I was hoping that book thieves would present more of a challenge," Rachel told Claire. "When you get right down to it, they weren't much smarter than any other thief."

Corinne went on living at the ranch with Mariah, Eric, and Pete. Mariah talked her into consulting a therapist and drove her into Tucson once a week. The estate was settled, and the property was deeded to Mariah. She had a DNA test to determine once and for all whether she was Burke's daughter, and it confirmed that her father was Benjamin deWitt. "I have no memory of him, and I feel like I'm Burke's daughter in spirit," she told Claire. In that spirit she ran the ranch as a nature preserve.

Jed Acker got Claire's message from the bartender in Reserve, and he called to apologize for his part in the conspiracy. The Stoners had sent him on a cattle-buying trip the weekend Claire was in the Blue and did not tell him she was coming. They played on his loyalties when they pressured him into signing the affidavit.

"Damned sorry," he told Claire. "My first loyalty should have been to Burke. I know he wanted the ranch to go to Mariah. This valley is getting to be an angry, uncomfortable place, and I'm thinking maybe its time for me to move on."

"Good luck," Claire said.

After the indictments came down, Claire and John Harlan went out to dinner to celebrate. He suggested she pick the place, and the place she chose was Scarpa's on Academy.

He looked at the menu and said, "Hell, Claire, what kind of pizza place is this? Santa Fe pizza with Kalamata olives and sun-dried tomatoes? Shrimp pizza with artichoke hearts and pesto? No cheese pizza? What kind of pizza has no cheese?"

"Try the spaghetti with meat sauce," Claire said.

"They can't do anything to spaghetti and meat sauce, can they?"

"I don't think so."

"I suppose you were smart enough to know all the time that the thief was Samantha," John said.

"I thought it was a good possibility," Claire replied. "But I didn't want to believe it."

"Now that you have the history back, what are you plannin' to do

195

with it? A murder was committed over that book. It could become the stuff of legend someday and worth a bundle. You should consider it a legacy for your children."

"How would anybody distinguish that copy of the history from any of the other copies? It didn't have a library stamp."

"It might have a on, ni, on ffep or ifc."

It sounded like a code from the personal ads, but Claire knew that he meant owner's name, name in ink on front free endpaper or inside front cover. In her mind, writing a name in a book defaced it.

"How many copies did Samantha have?" John asked.

"The police found ten in her house. Most had library stamps: one from Reserve, one from the U of A. They didn't find the center's copy. It could still be in the tower, mis-shelved somewhere. They found a copy marked in pencil with an *r y* on the inside front cover."

"That's mine."

"You'll have to prove it to the police if you want it back."

"No problem."

Book dealers use a code to remind themselves how much they paid for a book. Ordinarily they pick a word with ten different letters. The first letter in the word signifies that they paid one dollar, the second letter two dollars and so on. The first and second letter together would mean twelve. "What's your code word?" Claire asked John.

"You're askin' me to give away my secret code?"

"You may need my help to get your book back."

John looked down at the empty white tablecloth. "Ravenously," he said. "Which is kind of the way I feel right now."

"Your code word is . . . ravenously?"

"Why not? It's got ten different letters."

"The first is *r* and the last is *y*. So you paid ten dollars for the history?"

"Right."

"Your book could gain in value, too, if only for its proximity to the crime."

"Anything that increases a book's value is all right with me. What happened with the Austin/Adams folio?"

"The police got nowhere. Rusty wouldn't admit to knowing anything about it and neither would Reginald Arnold. The prints were long gone by the time the police got to the gallery."

"I'll bet they're hanging on somebody's wall in Santa Fe," John said.

"And Reginald's bank account has been enriched by more than I want to contemplate."

John's spaghetti arrived, and he began rolling it around on his fork. "Here's a question for you. Can you tell me when spaghetti became pasta?"

"I think it was 1972."

"A good year. Not many of us left who remember it. You didn't tell me what you're going to do with your *History of the Blue*." He put down his fork and watched her.

Claire saw dollar signs in his eyes. "Are you making me an offer?"

"Not exactly, but, hell, if you want to get rid of it, I'd be willing to help you out. That book might have some bad memories for you. Selling to me is one option."

Claire had considered the other options. She knew she'd never be comfortable coming home alone at night with the history in her house. She didn't want to see it in Harrison's office marked by the stamp of his ego. She feared that if it went to the tower it, too, would disappear. But she didn't want to sell it, no matter how much John was willing to pay. "It's in my safe deposit box," she said.

They lingered over coffee, then walked out to the parking lot to their cars. John waited while Claire inserted the key in her lock. "That was fun," he said. "We'll have to do it again sometime."

She looked over his shoulder and saw that the ghost of his deceased wife, Ellen, was becoming ever more ephemeral. "We will," she replied.